RYZEN

FEDERAL PROTECTION AGENCY

BOOK THREE

BY EVIE RILEY

RYZEN

True evil lurks in the darkness...

Recruited at eighteen by the CIA, Ryzen is one of the best snipers in the world. Now, he's working with the Federal Protection Agency to aid them in their fight to track down the vile people who perpetuate crimes against children. Always hidden behind his dark sunglasses, Ry is a mystery to everyone and he prefers it that way.

Ry remembers Knox from when he had his psych evaluation, and that the profiler's report was what resulted in his discharge from the CIA. He's not impressed with the man, and even more disturbed by the way he makes Ry feel.

A profiler with the FBI, Knox Hunter is investigating a series of murders. The victims are all male, between twelve and fourteen, and all have the same MO. With the Mayor pushing for re-election, a report of a serial killer could jeopardize the campaign's success, so Knox is sent in to work with the FPA to try and close the case, fast and by any means necessary. The only problem is, Knox is an office man, not a field man, and this new path could be the most dangerous one of his entire career.

Will Ry be able to keep Knox safe while they track down and put away this serial killer, or is he destined to be the biggest threat—to Knox's heart?

CHAPTER ONE

Knox

"WE FOUND HIM. He was dumped in a dumpster along Plank Road in between the twelve hundred and thirteen hundred blocks. A shop owner found him roughly an hour ago. I got a crime scene heading there now, and local PD has the scene blocked off."

That would be my boss, Special Agent

in Charge Greg Mathers. He was a short and stocky man, but that was only to fool you. The man looked like a short Santa Claus, making you believe he would be jolly and a fun elf. In reality, he was a mean son of a bitch that ran his unit with an iron fist. If you got on his bad side, well, let's just say you better start praying, whether you believe in a God or not.

I, thankfully, had never been on his bad side. I did my job and I did it to the best of my ability. As a FBI Profiler, my whole job was to analyze people, criminals mostly, and study their behavior. It was on me to find killers, sex offenders, arsonists, and any number of other dangerous felons to get them off of the street and into prison where they belonged. I loved my job and I was one of the best profilers in the country. I knew that fact was the only thing saving my ass from getting tossed overboard by my boss.

For the past three months, I had been working on the same case. Three months of me trying to find one single person in a city of just over two hundred thousand. It sounds insane, but when you are used to finding one single person in an entire country, it really should be nothing. I was one of the best profilers, I had all of the accommodations and solve rate to prove it.

So why the hell couldn't I find this son of a bitch?

I was working on a series of murders with the victims between the ages of twelve and fourteen. All were male. All had been kidnapped and tortured. No signs of sexual assault, so it wasn't a pedophile kidnapping and killing young teenage boys. They were all grabbed and killed within seventy-two hours before being dumped. There were now twelve victims. My killer had a one week timeframe, so not much of a cooling off period. We had a serial killer in Baton Rouge, and it was one targeting young teenage males, putting close to fifteen thousand kids at risk of being kidnapped.

I was spinning my wheels with this case. There didn't appear to be anything connecting the twelve victims. They didn't go to the same school. They didn't go to the same church. They were all with different religions and extracurricular activities. Some came from a perfect, two parent household, and others were in foster care. Different dentists, different doctors, different areas of the city. They didn't look the same. Nothing was the same. It was as if the killer was going out of his way to pick the most random kids possible. And even then, it wasn't random. He wasn't grabbing the kids at the first available opportunity. He was watching them and learning their patterns. He knew when to strike and grab them so he wouldn't be seen. He wasn't caught on camera at the abduction site or the dumping site. The dumping was always in a dumpster, but in a city this size, it wasn't like we could stake out each dumpster.

My boss was frustrated, but so was I.

"I don't want to admit this, but I have nothing. I have no idea who he is or how he is connected to them. I'm spinning my wheels on this one, Boss. We really need to tell the public. These kids need to be warned. Their parents need to be warned."

You would think with now twelve murdered boys that it would be all over the media. It wasn't. The Mayor had issued a gag order to all media outlets to not report what had been happening. Nowhere in the press would you be able to hear or read about these boys.

At least, not yet.

I had done that before in other cities when I traveled to help local law enforcement with solving their cases. Sometimes it was better to not report the crimes. For two reasons, the first, it makes the unknown subject, or UnSub as we call them, think they are safe and no one is looking for them. With that perception of safety, they keep making mistakes, and they don't run, so we can grab them. The second, a lot of the time these UnSubs like the attention they get from the media. They want to be known, they want to go down in history. By stopping that from happening, they get angry and they make a mistake.

That's wasn't the case here, though.

Nope, the Mayor was up for re-election and what does not get you re-elected is broadcasting about a serial killer that targets young males and had been killing and torturing them for three months, now. That didn't look good on a campaign poster, and like a true politician, she was opting for saving her own ass and not the people she is supposed to serve.

"You know that won't happen. The Mayor is not going to lift the gag order, so I suggest you find out who this son of a bitch is. This is the only case you are going to be working and you won't be working it alone."

"I appreciate the offer of help, Boss, but too many profilers in one kitchen is not a good idea."

It wasn't that I was against working a case with someone. The opposite in fact, I loved working with different law enforcement. What I did not love was working with other profilers. As a profiler, your job is to analyze everything, it's programmed into your mind. We all tend to have a degree in Behavioral Science, putting us within the psychologist category. We examine every word, movement, or look that someone gives, and we evaluate them based on that.

And I do mean everyone.

I did it just this morning with my Barista who kept eyeing her co-worker when he wasn't looking. She liked him and he had no clue.

A typical man in that sense.

But everywhere I go, my brain is always on, just like most profilers. Which is exactly the problem with working with them. They analyze your every movement, look, and word spoken. They over-analyze every tiny detail and when you get more than one in a room, it becomes a debate on everything. They always think they are right and everyone else is wrong. I don't have that issue. I have no problem with brainstorming and seeing what puzzle pieces we can put together, but it's exhausting having to play referee in a room full of grown ass adults.

"I didn't say you were working with other profilers on this. There's a new Agency in town. They got here about a month ago. They have made a name for themselves within the community already. The Federal Protection Agency, they focus on crimes against children. They have put an end to an enormous human trafficking ring, have cleaned up the foster care system in parts of Maryland, and they have been working closely with DCFS to help clean up the foster care system here and try and locate kids that have been scooped up by the human traffickers. They have already started to generate reputation in the community for being able to stop criminals that go after children. The team has been given immunity by the Governor of Maryland, who then, had it transferred over here in an agreement with our Governor. If there's anyone that can get this case solved, and quietly, it's them."

I had heard about the small waves the FPA had been making since they got into town. It never bothered me that they were here, but I knew some of the other Feds had an issue with it. They didn't like that the Agency was made up of Feds and local police from out of state. From what I had heard, they also had a couple private detectives that worked with them as well. It was random people put together, but it was somehow working. They had been able to do some good since getting here.

Still, I wasn't certain on the keeping it quiet part.

They had immunity, which meant they didn't have to answer to the Mayor. They could do whatever they wanted, scream about the murders from a rooftop, should they think it was best. Their immunity protected them from a gag order.

But then, maybe that was Mathers' point.

Take the case to someone that didn't have to play politics. Someone that could blow it wide open to the public and maybe force my UnSub to be smarter. Either way, I was good with the offered help.

"I'll head over there with my case files. I want to go to the scene first and make sure it is secured."

"Make sure you stay within the perimeter and if you need to leave it, you have an officer with you."

"Copy, Boss," I easily agreed.

He headed out and I quickly grabbed all of my case files for all twelve victims. I would need to add to this victim's file, but I could do that in the car once I visited the dump site. With everything set, I headed out for my car. With being a profiler my job was mostly in the office. It wasn't very often I would go to a crime scene or chase after a suspect. Sometimes, I would go to the scene to get my own view of it, but most of the time I could go off of the photos and videos taken by the lead detective.

Whenever a victim or a loved one of the victim needed to be spoken to, they mostly came into the station where I was working at the time. It wasn't often I had to go out to them. I wasn't a field agent. I didn't have a gun. I didn't have any formal combat training. I was the brains of the operation and not the muscle, and that was perfectly fine with me.

I worked out to stay in shape. Working out was my stress relief. It helped to go the gym and clear my mind when I was stuck on a case. So, physically it looked like I could fight, but honestly, I had never thrown a single punch before in my life. That wasn't the life that I had, even when I was younger.

My parents were great people. It was just the three of us so I didn't have any older brothers I had to fight against. We lived in a good area. I went to a private school and played on the chess team. I went to Harvard with a full scholarship for my Behavioral Science Degree.

I had a really good life growing up.

A life that didn't involve violence or pain.

I knew I was one of the lucky ones and I never took it for granted, especially since I had been working as a profiler for the past fourteen years. The greatest weapon I had was my mind and I didn't see the need to end a situation with more violence, not if I could talk the UnSub down.

Once I arrived at the scene, I parked my vehicle in the area of the other patrol cars and climbed out. I could already see the locals gathering around to watch the scene unfold. It was a common occurrence with crime scenes.

The human mind always wants to learn and know information. When someone is killed or even when the police show up, everyone is always looking out their windows to see what is going on. Part of human nature was being nosy and gossiping. Something like this would be talked about for a couple of weeks, at least.

The area itself was a mixture of old businesses and rundown homes that had been converted into one or two apartments. The area was in the higher crime rate within the city. They weren't strangers to police cars in the streets and I knew the prostitutes and drug dealers would be laying low for the next couple of days until the police presence disappeared. Then they could go back to making money.

What I also knew, though, was no one would talk. There would be no witnesses, not even when you told them it was a young teenage boy. They didn't talk in this area, too controlled and afraid of the gangs that would kill anyone who dared to speak to a cop or a Fed.

"Special Agent Hunter," I said, holding up my badge as I walked onto the crime scene. "Who is in charge of the scene?" I glanced around at the local PD officers standing around the area.

"That would be me, Detective Jonah West with Homicide. What can I do for you, Special Agent?"

"The FBI have been working a case and your victim is connected to an ongoing investigation that I have been running. The FBI will take over the case. I would appreciate it if you could send me your notes and any of the crime scene photos."

"Look, I got no problem sharing, but I'm not about to hand over this case fully to you. That's a twelve year old boy in that dumpster. Someone left him there like trash after torturing him. I'm not going to hand it over to anyone, Fed or not."

It was always hard to convince local law enforcement to give up a case, especially when it involved children. I could tell he had a child, probably a boy around the same age. The passion within him was not going to go away overnight. This would be a case he was going to keep a close eye on and make sure it got solved. I understood that and I completely respected it.

"I understand you don't want to give this case up. However, I have jurisdiction over you. If necessary, I can very simply call your boss and order it be handed over. I can't tell you about an ongoing investigation, however, I can tell you that I will be working with the Federal Protection Agency to get this case solved. We will get who did this and they will go to jail for the rest of their natural life. And I promise you, I will keep you updated and informed throughout."

I didn't want to have to pull rank. Pulling rank always left a bad taste in my mouth and it did nothing to help improve working relations with local police. However, I also couldn't allow him to work this case and potentially release information that was under the gag order. I also wasn't convinced it would be ideal to broadcast that we had a serial killer. I wasn't certain which direction this UnSub would go if he was dragged out into the light. I needed to figure him out more first.

"I'll make sure everything gets sent your way," he said in a tight voice.

"Thank you, Detective West. I truly appreciate it," I offered, flashing him a warm smile.

The Detective ignored me and turned on his heel, walking away.

Well, I wasn't making a new friend out of him, but at least I had control of the case. Once I finished up here, I would make my way to the new Agency's field office and, hopefully, we would finally be able to get something on this case to bring us closer to our UnSub.

The clock was already ticking on the next victim. If we didn't want another kid to die, we had seven days to stop this killer.

I just hoped we would make it in time.

CHAPTER TWO

Ryzen

"MORNING," ROLAND SAID as he walked into the conference room.

I just gave him a nod. We were going to be going over potential cases to work this morning and I was hoping for a good one. Not that there could really be a *good one* when you were dealing with crimes against children, but to me, if we could shut down another organization that was hurting a great deal of children, that was a good one. I was all for saving as many children at one time as possible.

"Are you ever going to talk to me?" Roland asked with a teasing smile.

I was quiet, everyone knew that. What they didn't know, was that it was programmed into me. Growing up, if they couldn't hear you, you couldn't be hurt. It was all about survival and it stuck with me. Besides, I didn't have anything interesting to say most of the time. I didn't have many social skills, even at the age of thirty.

I had never been to school, not grade school or high school. But that's what happens when you grow up in war torn areas of Africa following a mission around. There was never a time for me to be able to go to school. I learned from the people in the mission and that translated to taking care of various injuries and shooting. There wasn't any need to learn history, science, geography, or English literature. The one thing I could do better than your average person was math, but that went into my trade craft. If you want to be one of the best snipers within the world, you better be able to do advanced math in your head at a moment's notice.

"Hi," I said back.

"There we go, progress," Roland said, and flashed me a warm smile.

"Tyler?"

I knew Roland and Tyler were having a bit of a harder time adjusting to the long-distance relationship they found themselves in. Over the past two months, we could tell that Roland was missing him. Their relationship hadn't grown in a typical sense. More often than not people had a grace period of six months or even years before they moved in with someone. Roland and Tyler were practically living together almost right away. They had to learn how to live apart now, and not just in the same town, but a four hour plane ride or seventeen hour car ride away from each other. They had to go from seeing one another 24/7 to only video calls and text messages.

Tyler had said he wasn't ready for a move like the rest of us had made, and that made sense. He had a whole life he was still trying to piece together. He was young, he had a lot left to learn about himself, and for the first time, he had a stable job and a home, plus friends in Gaithersburg. I knew, eventually, he would move down here to Baton Rouge to be with Roland, though. You could tell they deeply loved the other. Still, it was likely the waiting was going to take a toll on both of them, especially Roland.

"He's doing good. He's decided to get his GED. He's thinking about the future and maybe even going to college one day. He's been working with the occupational therapist to help him with his reading. He's doing really well and building up some confidence in himself," Roland said with a proud smile.

Tyler has dyslexia, just like Mason. Though unlike Mason, Tyler didn't have anyone growing up to diagnose him or to help him rewire his brain so he could read. Roland had helped Mason with it growing up and I knew he had been helping Tyler as well. The only time you could tell that Mason even had a learning disability was when he had been up for too many days straight. That's when his ability to read went to shit. It never bothered us, though. There were plenty of us that could read a report for him. And wasn't exactly like he needed to be able to read to shoot straight.

"Here before the Boss, must have a new case," Cooper said as he strolled in with his extra large coffee. The man was going to have a heart attack one day from all the caffeine he drank.

"I wonder what it is," Hollingsworth said as he sat down beside Rafe.

Jarod strode into the room.

"He got a call early this morning from someone in the FBI. Whatever is going on has to be big enough that the FBI is looking for our help," Jarod informed us as he slid into his usual seat.

Mason and Jarod were still going strong. They had their own place together and you would often see them and Koda everywhere. Where one went, the other two generally did. I was happy for them, even if I didn't show it. I was happy for all of the guys. They had started to become my brothers and I wanted them to be happy and in great relationships.

And speaking of relationships.

"How's Lilly and Fin?" I asked Rafe. The two newest members of our misfit family. Fin was the younger brother of Rafe's best friend, John, who had been murdered in a home invasion. Lilly, John's daughter, who is six now, had been kidnapped when she was five by a human trafficking organization. The same organization who had killed Fin's brother.

Fin had gone undercover to find her.

When Rafe got word about the whole situation, he decided he was going undercover with Fin to shut them down and find Lilly. We all went down to help and brought everyone home successfully.

When we were all relocated to Baton Rouge with the Federal Protection Agency task force, Fin and Lilly made the move with Rafe and they had been living together for the past two months. They lived in a house in a gated community with rolling guards 24/7. It might sound extreme, but it made Fin and Lilly feel safer and that was all that Rafe cared about.

"They are doing really well. They are both going through therapy and Lilly is doing well with the support group she is in. She has a hard time being around men still, and she's plagued with nightmares almost every night, but she is able to play during the day and be a normal six year old, for the most part. We're thinking about getting her a service dog. Her therapist recommended it and Mason said it could really help her."

"I know a lot of Veterans who have PTSD dogs that have helped them a great deal, especially with being around people," Roland said.

"Same, that's what I told him. We're gonna look around and see what puppies are available from the local service dog breeders. See which one she would like and what breed would be easier. Thankfully, they didn't use dogs in the trafficking organization so she's not scared of them," Rafe commented.

"When we've gone around with Koda,

she lights up when he's there. I think it'll be good for her," Jarod added.

I wasn't a huge fan of dogs. I could handle being around them, but I wasn't a dog person. I had been bit by a dog a few times growing up, from either one of the wild dogs in Africa or by one of the guard dogs that the Rebels had. I was fine around Koda, though. He was a good dog and he listened to whatever command you gave him. But that didn't mean I wanted to hang out with Koda all day long, or any other dog for that matter.

The clicking on the floor told us that Koda was coming down the hallway and that meant Mason would be as well. Hopefully, this case wouldn't be too hard to shut down. Koda came into the room first followed by Mason, but then everything went to shit when *he* walked into the room.

Fucking Special Agent Knox Hunter.

The man responsible for the end of my career. He was a Profiler, supposedly one of the best within the Country. Before being let go, I had worked for the CIA since I was eighteen. They had scooped me up right out of Africa for my shooting ability. There wasn't anything I couldn't hit, from any distance. I was gifted where a gun was concerned. Five years ago, the CIA decided they needed to make sure I was mentally sound after killing people over half of my life. Knox was the Profiler that was picked to evaluate me. According to him, I was too mentally unstable, due to a personality disorder, to be capable of making a right and wrong decision. That it would be best for the Agency and the Country for me to no longer be working as a sniper. According to Knox, I wasn't able to see the difference between right and wrong and it was only a matter of time before I became a black hat sniper and started to go against the Agency.

And just like that, the CIA kicked me to the curb.

Sure, I could have taken on contracts and become a black hat sniper. Gone after anybody and everybody that had a high price tag on their head. Instead, though, I continued to be a white hat sniper and take out targets that other Federal Agencies all over the world didn't have the skills to do. I had done freelance work. *Legal* freelance work.

Knox had a firm belief in good and evil, black and white, but the world didn't work that way and that was what he failed to see. The world was made up of millions of shades of grey and what works in one situation doesn't always work in the next. Sometimes, you have to do something questionable and not fully legal in order to take a dangerous threat out of the world.

Knox had no idea what true horrors there were out in the world. Even working as a Profiler and handling murder cases, he still didn't get it. I'd bet my ass he grew up in a perfect house with perfect parents and had the perfect childhood and adulthood. He'd never had to fight for his life. He'd never had to feel his stomach eating itself for weeks because there wasn't even a scrap of food to eat. He'd never had to eat literal garbage to survive. He had no idea just how fucked up this world really was.

All *I* knew was how horrible the world

was.

I knew all about the evil that lived in plain sight. Some of the worst criminals there were lived right out in the open for the whole world to see, but no one ever did. Everyone was just happy to live with blinders on and pretend like the world wasn't going to complete shit.

Guys like Knox.

"All right, listen up. This is Special Agent Knox Hunter. He is a Profiler with the local FBI Field Office. He has been working a case for three months now, and we are being asked to assist," Mason started.

"What's the case?" Roland immediately piped up.

Knox's gaze had fixated on me the moment he walked into the room and was still on me. I could tell he was trying to figure out how the hell I was here. I guess he assumed that after being kicked out of the CIA, I would go and crawl into some hole. Or maybe, he expected to be chasing me down one day. Joke was on him, I was still a Fed. I was still doing what I was born to do.

"Agent Hunter," Mason said, and that seemed to snap Knox out of it.

I couldn't help but smirk at his clear discomfort.

"Right, um... I have been chasing a serial killer for the past three months," Knox started, but Rafe cut him off.

"Wait, we haven't heard anything about a serial killer in the press."

"It's a re-election year. Part of the Mayor's campaign is the crime rate going down. This would prove otherwise," Knox stated.

"But the crime rate isn't going down," Hollingsworth pointed out.

"It is in certain areas. Areas in the city that cater to middle and upper classes of society. Those numbers have gone down, while other crimes are either not being reported, or they are being swept under the rug to pad the crime rates. People will believe the numbers and not realize that violent crimes have, in fact, been going up in certain areas of the city. The Mayor has placed a gag order on the press, so they can't report anything until it's been lifted."

That was the problem with politicians. They only cared about being elected. They didn't care about the people they were supposed to be serving. They didn't care about protecting people. If there was a serial killer for the past three months, then the city should've be made aware of it so the potential victims would be on alert, know that they were potentially at risk. It was bullshit.

"Why are we getting brought in?" Jarod asked.

"The UnSub, the killer, he's killed twelve people so far, one a week for the past three months. He is targeting males between the ages of twelve and fourteen. The twelfth victim was just found a couple of hours ago. All were kidnapped and then dead within seventy-two hours. They were all tortured before death, but no signs of sexual assault."

And that is why he was coming to us. We focused on crimes against children and a serial killer was a major crime against children. This UnSub wouldn't stop until he was caught or killed. My vote was to be killed. A man like that deserved to die and not get to live the rest of his life in a jail cell.

"Any connections between the victims?" Mason asked.

"Nothing. I have gone through their entire lives, and the parents, there is no nexus. They appear to be chosen completely at random. I have all of the case files with me. I haven't spoken to the latest victim's parents just yet."

"All right, everyone, divide and conquer. I want the names divided up and let's dig into their lives, into their friends' lives, both kids and parents. Coop, see if you can find the same MO in the database, maybe he was in another State before moving here. Serial killers don't pop up overnight. He had to have other victims from when he first started,"

Mason instructed.

"Based on my profile, he is a single male, most likely white, and appears non-threatening. He's getting the kids to go with him somehow, and my best guess is without force. No one heard any screams or cries for help from his victims when they were grabbed. Serial killers are born or made, and we need to know which one he is to better understand him. There will be signs in his childhood and early adult life, whether that is animal cruelty, setting fires, or assault. His first victim would've been someone close to him and it would have been unorganized and messy. If we can figure out who his first victim was, there might be evidence that was collected from the body or the crime scene that could connect us to him," Knox added.

"Coop, do your thing. Ry, you go with Knox to the latest victim's house," Mason ordered.

"I'll stay," I said, hopefully making it clear to everyone that I wanted nothing to do with Knox. I'd never defied an order before so they had to know something was up.

"Okay, I don't know what happened between the two of you and I don't care. Knox is not cleared to be in the field alone, he has no combat training or a weapon. Until this UnSub is caught, Ryzen, he's your new partner and it's on you to keep him alive. You're the best shooter and field agent we have. So grab your gear and head out."

The very last thing I wanted to do was go anywhere with this asshole, but Mason wasn't going to let me get out of it. Knox couldn't be in the field alone, and with my skills, I was the best person to make sure he didn't get himself killed. What Mason failed to realize, was that I didn't give two flying shits if Knox got himself killed.

And I sure as shit wasn't taking a bullet for his ass.

I got up and headed out of the room at a brisk walk. If Knox wanted to follow me that was his choice, I didn't care. The sooner this case was wrapped up, the better, and not just for the young males in town. The sooner I got Knox the fuck out of my life, the better off I would be.

CHAPTER THREE

Knox

I COULDN'T BELIEVE my luck. Out of all the people they could have in their agency, they picked Ryzen. How the hell he even wormed his way onto the Federal Protection Agency was beyond me. Clearly, there hadn't been an interview or screening process, because otherwise they never would have picked him.

Agent Wright didn't appear to be that incompetent that he would allow a man like Ryzen to be in an agency dedicated to protecting children. The man saw no line in the sand. To him, everyone deserved to be killed. The world was nothing but darkness and there were no good people left in it. The man had no morals or any beliefs. Nothing that would keep a man from doing harm to the innocent people in the world. On top of that, he had one of the highest kill rates I had ever seen. If he hadn't been working for the CIA, he would be considered a mass murderer and being hunted himself to be put down.

This was ridiculous.

He had been fired from the CIA after I filed my evaluation on him. I was thrilled to hear that he had been let go. He needed to be kept away from guns for the rest of his life. However, I knew he was angry about it and it wouldn't surprise me at all if he pulled a gun and shot me in the back of the head the first chance he got.

And don't even get me started on his personality, or the lack of one. The man barely spoke to me while I was doing his evaluation. He just sat there with the same stupid sunglasses on.

Who the hell wears sunglasses inside?

Even today he had them on, it was ridiculous and completely rude. A person deserved the respect of being able to look you in the eyes. It was common courtesy to offer that respect to everyone we spoke to, inside or outside. It was as if basic social manners had never been taught to him and he never bothered to learn them. I had no idea what his childhood was like, but I had arrested men with his psychopathy for arson and serial killings.

Ryzen was a ticking time bomb just waiting to explode.

And now, I was truly expected to have him around me. I didn't need a babysitter. No, I wasn't a field agent, but I didn't need anyone to go with me to talk to the parents of a victim. I didn't need someone slowing me down.

I didn't know what Agent Wright was thinking partnering us up. He clearly knew there was a problem between us, and that right there should have been a red flag for him. He should have placed me with someone else and kept Ryzen far away from this case and from me.

I spoke, breaking the silence between us, as we pulled up to the latest victim's house. "Don't mention the gag order or the fact that it's a serial killer. It would be best for you to not speak at all. Which shouldn't be an issue for you."

As I got out, I just faintly heard Ryzen's voice. "You talk enough for the both of us."

He actually said it faintly, under his breath, so there was an actual chance I wouldn't hear him. Like we were twelve and trying to pass insults to each other without the other hearing it. It was only further proof how unprofessional and childish he was. Hopefully, this would be the only time I had to deal with him.

I made my way to the front door and rang the doorbell. I was pleased to see that there weren't any reporters out front. I knew local PD had notified the parents already. I had hoped they would already have had a chance to get over the initial shock and pain and be calm enough for us to talk. It wasn't that I had a hard time with grieving loved ones, it was that we were on a clock this time, and if the clock ran out another child could die.

The door opened a minute later to reveal Mr. Burnsworth. His eyes were red and his clothes were disheveled. He had allegedly been worrying about his son for seventy-two hours, give or take, ever since they had discovered the boy had been kidnapped.

Standard practice is for the parents to wait by the phone and be there for a ransom demand. What most didn't understand was three quarters of the time a ransom call never came. When a child is grabbed, it's more often than not for a sexual reason and it often results in the child being kept or killed. It all depended on the UnSub and what they were looking for and if the child could provide it for them.

"Mr. Burnsworth, I'm Special Agent Hunter and this is my associate, Ryzen. I hoped to speak with you and your wife about your son, Kevin."

That was another thing that drove me absolutely insane. It was always just *Ryzen*. There was never a last name attached to it, not even in the CIA file that I was given. Now yes, the file was heavily redacted, but his name was clear as day. There was no last name on file. As if he decided to wake up one day and be like Cher. It was infuriating.

"Of course. Please, come in," Mr. Burnsworth said as he moved back to allow us to enter his home.

The house itself was very nice. We

were in one of the suburbs that catered to higher income families. I knew from the quick research that I did, that Mr. Burnsworth was a doctor and his wife was a stay at home mom. They lived within their means and they didn't have any criminal background or debt. There were no signs of marital problems online, but I knew online and in real life were often two very different things. They appeared to be loving and doting parents to Kevin. They'd reported him missing within an hour of him failing to show up when he said he would. He had been at a friend's house and had left at seven at night three nights ago. He was to be home by eight and it was only a twenty-minute walk. The area was a nice area so they felt like it was safe enough for their twelve year old to walk home alone. Not that I could blame them, he should have been more than safe.

We were guided to the living room where Mrs. Burnsworth was sitting on the couch. Ryzen didn't remove his sunglasses and I swear it took everything in me to not rip them right off from his face. I swore I was going to do it one day.

I sat down on the chair across from the grieving couple as Ryzen started to wander around the living room. I didn't care what he was doing, it was no business of mine as long as he stayed quiet and didn't break anything.

"Mr. and Mrs. Burnsworth, I'm sorry to have to put you through this, but there's some questions I need to ask you about your son," I started.

"We understand. We just want whoever is responsible to pay. You go ahead and ask your questions," Mr. Burnsworth said with as much strength as he could manage.

"Have either of you received any threats within the past few months?" I started.

"No," Mr. Burnsworth answered, and looked at me quizzically, furrowing his brow.

"What about Kevin? Anyone at school bullying him or was there someone you noticed had been hanging around him?"

"No, nothing like that. The school doesn't tolerate bullies and we're all a close-knit neighborhood. We look out for each other's children. No one has even moved in within the past two years," Mr. Burnsworth answered again.

"Have you had any work done recently on your home?"

The UnSub had to have gotten to the children somehow. I just couldn't figure out how. I needed that nexus to be able to pinpoint who this UnSub could be. I needed the nexus to start to form a list of suspects. Until I had it, I had nothing to go off of and I hated feeling like a failure or useless, especially when children's lives were on the line.

"No, the house was built brand new when we purchased the land five years ago. We haven't had anyone do any repairs or inspections. Nothing new has been installed since we moved in," Mr. Burnsworth answered.

"He's not yours," Ryzen said, before I could get a chance to ask another question.

I snapped my head around at his words just as the Burnsworths snapped their heads up at him. I didn't know if I was more horrified or pissed by what he just said. Of all the things to say to grieving parents, he had the audacity to state that their child wasn't theirs. We needed the parents to work with us. We needed them on our side, and attacking them like this, making that kind of statement, was only going to do the opposite. I could see the anger swirling within both the Burnsworths' eyes. They wanted to rip Ryzen a new one and I was inclined to allow it to happen.

"Excuse me? What right do you have to come into my home and say that to me?" Mrs. Burnsworth asked with tears building up in her eyes.

"I'm sorry for what my associate has said. He's still trying to learn decent human behavior," I said with a pointed look at Ryzen, hoping he would get the message and shut the hell up.

"I meant no disrespect, ma'am. Your whole family took a picture, uncles, aunts, grandparents, but all of them have brown hair and brown eyes. Kevin has blond hair and blue eyes. Biologically, he can't be yours."

Holy shit.

If Kevin was adopted, then maybe that was the nexus. Maybe the other kids were adopted as well. That opened up a lot of possibilities that I could work with. There were social workers, therapists, and people working in family court that would have access to those records. The UnSub could be targeting them for one reason or another.

If that was true, then the UnSub might be adopted.

"Yes, he's adopted. Kevin has known since he was five when he asked why he was different to everyone else. He's been fine with it, though," Mrs. Burnsworth stated.

"The adoption, was it open or closed?" I asked.

Now this was exciting. This was something new. Not all adoptions were available to be viewed, even by law enforcement. You had to petition a judge to unlock the records. We would need to run the kid's names with a family court judge to see if they popped in their system. Then petition the court to get the records unsealed.

"Closed. We met Kevin's biological mother when she was seven months pregnant. She was fifteen and wasn't ready to be a mother. We offered to have it set as open, but she felt it would be easier for her to let him go if she couldn't see him. It would be easier for her to heal and we've always respected her wishes," Mr. Burnsworth answered.

"Do you know her name?" I asked.

"No, she only told us to call her Amanda. She wanted to remain as anonymous as possible. I always got the feeling that she was worried about her parents. She carried a rosary and a Bible all the time. I got the impression that it would be best for her and her family to act as if it never even happened," Mrs. Burnsworth stated.

That wasn't uncommon. The biological parents didn't have to give their full name to the adopting parents if they didn't wish to. They could remain completely anonymous, should they choose. The system never cared because they were focused on the child and not the biological parents.

I pulled out the line up of the previous eleven victims. I had carried the string of photos around with me as each new victim presented themselves. These were their school photos and not their death photos. I placed the strip of eleven photographs down on the coffee table in front of the couple as I spoke.

"Do either of you recognize any of these boys?"

They both looked at the photos, but I could tell they had no idea who they were. I had hoped that maybe one set of victim's parents would recognize someone in the line up. Someone that could give us a place to search. Knowing that Kevin was adopted was a huge win today.

"No, I'm sorry, we don't. Who are they?" Mr. Burnsworth asked.

"I'm not at liberty to speak about an on-going investigation. I was just curious if maybe you recognized any of them."

"Why adoption?" Ryzen asked as he came and stood next to the chair I was currently sitting in. There was a free chair; he should have sat. It was like wolves raised him.

"I wasn't able to conceive a baby. My doctor had said my egg count was too low and it would be basically impossible to get pregnant. We wanted to have a family and it didn't matter to us if the child was biologically ours," Mrs. Burnsworth answered.

I pulled out a pad of paper and handed it over to them along with a pen as I spoke, "Could you write down the name of the adoption agency, who you spoke with there, and anyone that you can remember who was involved in the adoption process. I'll also need the name of your physician, at the time, who recommended you try adoption, please."

"If you think it'll help," Mrs. Bursnworth said as she took the offered items.

"Why the interest?" Mr. Burnsworth asked.

"In a case like this, it's better to have too much information rather than not enough. We know someone you all know didn't take your son. And we know there was no ransom demand, so it wasn't about money. Money that you both clearly have. Kevin was taken for another reason, and now that we know he was adopted, he could have been targeted for that very reason. It would be helpful to have the information so we can verify the alibis of everyone that knew he was adopted outside of your circle of family and friends," I explained.

I knew it would have been simpler to just tell them it was because we were chasing a serial killer, but I couldn't break the gag order. And in this situation, I wasn't certain it would bring any comfort to them to know that he had been killed so horribly. As it stood, they just knew he was killed. They didn't know about the torture and it should stay that way for as long as possible.

Once the list was completed, I pulled out my card and handed it to them as I spoke, "We won't take up anymore of your time. I am truly sorry for your loss. If you have any questions or if you remember something, please don't hesitate to call me."

"Thank you," Mr. Burnsworth said.

I stood and we both headed out, leaving the parents to grieve in privacy. This was going to be something that affected them for the rest of their lives. I knew I had to find their son's killer or they would never be able to properly move on from this. There was no chance of moving on if there was never justice.

We climbed into Ryzen's car and drove back to the station. This time around, I didn't care that the car ride was completely silent, not even the radio played, further proof that something was seriously wrong with this man.

My mind was too busy asking questions that I knew were going to take time to answer. I was okay with that, though, because now, I had questions that could receive answers. I had a chance of being able to discover answers that could lead us to the UnSub.

This case had finally hit its first serious lead and it was one that I was hoping would pay off. Yes, if they were all adopted there would be a lot of suspects, both old and new, working within the adoption circuit, but having too many suspects was a hell of a lot better than the zero we were currently facing. I pulled out my phone and called Mason. He answered after two rings.

"You're on speaker."

"We just discovered that Kevin Burnsworth was adopted as an infant. It was a closed adoption. We need to run the other victims' names to see if any of them were adopted as well."

"Coop, pause what you are doing and start running the names. We need to see how many pop," Mason said before he spoke to me again. "It could be a one-off, but we might get lucky and find a soft connection."

"I'm hoping the majority were adopted and that could point us in some direction that we could use to generate suspects. With every new piece of information that we get, it makes it easier for me to build a realistic profile of our UnSub and we can then cross reference the profile with potential suspects. He's killing one a week, so we only have seven days to stop him before he grabs someone else."

"We'll have the names run before you get back. We'll keep working the cases and re-examining all of the evidence. Nice find, guys."

"Thanks."

I ended the call and I couldn't help but be slightly annoyed. The *nice find* was from Ryzen and it hurt a great deal for me to admit it. He had noticed the difference when my mind didn't even register that Kevin's parents had brown eyes and hair. Of course they wouldn't be able to have a blond hair, blue-eyed baby. Genetically, it wasn't possible.

This was the one time I was glad that Ryzen didn't have any desire to talk, the very last thing I wanted to hear out of his mouth was I told you so.

"Nice work, Profiler," he commented, disgust lacing his voice at the mention of my title.

Asshole.

CHAPTER FOUR

Ryzen

OF COURSE KNOX wasn't going to give me any credit for giving us the first real lead he'd had in a case he'd been working for three months. I still couldn't believe it. Three months he'd been working this serial killer case, twelve victims, child victims, and he had jack shit. He was supposed to be one of the best profilers in the country and he couldn't even find one serial killer in his own town.

It was ridiculous, and it only further fueled my anger toward him.

This was the guy that had cost me my position in the CIA. He was a hack and it was just that simple. The sooner I got him out of my life, the better off I would be.

I forced my thoughts to go back to this case. I could tell right away that Kevin was adopted by looking at his parents. I wanted to scan the photos, though, to confirm there wasn't anyone else in the family with blond hair and blue eyes. Families could have a mixture of hair and eye color, but when it was a dominant gene that every family member had on both sides, there was no way Kevin wouldn't have inherited it. The only way for him to have blond hair and blue eyes was for him to be adopted. I wasn't a geneticist, but I knew quite a bit about genetics.

I always wore my sunglasses because the lights hurt my eyes. It was a side effect from having grey eyes. It was one of the rarest eye colors there was and it was from a hereditary gene mutation. The lack of melanin in my eyes meant my eyes were unprotected from the harsh UV rays from the sun. The sunglasses helped protect my eyes from potentially developing eye cancer. Plus, any bright light hurt them.

It was a real bitch when I lived in Africa.

When I arrived back in the States when I was eighteen, I had gone to see an eye doctor. He advised me of the specialty sunglasses that I should wear to help protect my eyes. There were no cancer signs back then and the glasses would help to, hopefully, prevent eye cancer from developing. Other than the light sensitivity, my eyesight was perfect.

I knew people had questions about why I always wore the sunglasses, even indoors or on a rainy day. It wasn't any of their business, though. Even the lights at my house were all low wattages, including the fridge light. I also had headaches from too many concussions and a couple of skull fractures, so the low light helped to prevent any headaches or migraines from glares on reflective surfaces.

The Burnsworths, their reactions looked genuine. They were genuinely grieving their son, which made me believe they weren't involved, and if they suspected anyone, they would have given them up. They weren't looking to protect anyone that could have done this to their son. They seemed like nice people.

And that was the shitty part in all of this.

They had done something nice, adopted a child that could have been abused through the foster system. They provided a loving home with toys, books, food, clothing, everything a child needed to survive and feel loved. They had endless family photos of trips, holidays, and sporting events that Kevin clearly participated in. They had his report cards framed, for fuck's sake. They were good people that provided a loving and safe home for a child. And here they were mourning the loss of their son who had been kidnapped and brutally murdered.

It wasn't fair, but that was life and I

learned that a long time ago.

The second we arrived back at the Agency, Knox jumped out of my car before I even shifted to park, and all but sprinted for the door.

I followed behind him and made my way up to the conference room. We had turned an old office building into our own agency field office. We each had our own offices, we had a couple of conference rooms, interview rooms, there was a kitchen, a lounge area with a TV, and even a ping-pong table. We also had a holding area built with cells to keep any suspects on site. There was plenty of room left to expand, and I knew Mason hoped to grow with more techs and Agents so we could work multiple cases at one time. I was all for expanding if that meant we could help more people.

"Good, you're back. So far, Cooper has been able to confirm five of the other children were put up for adoption. The records are sealed, though," Mason stated.

"And the others weren't?" Knox asked.

"Don't know. I can't find them, but that doesn't mean they weren't adopted. Not everyone is placed on the adoption registry. You'd have to call a family court judge or a federal prosecutor with enough pull to run their names," Cooper answered.

"I got a guy," I said as I pulled out my phone.

"What guy?" Rafe asked, clearly shocked.

These guys always seemed to forget that I had a life before them. I had plenty of different contacts that I could reach out to for information or help, should I need it. I'd worked for every agency in this world and that brought a lot of connections in both the legal and illegal worlds.

"Federal prosecutor," I said as I headed for the door to make the call in private.

"Of course you have a lawyer," Knox said, and I knew he wasn't impressed. Though, he probably figured I needed a lawyer so often I had one on speed dial.

I headed down the hallway a short distance to reach my office. I closed the door as I hit Noah's name on my phone.

Noah Riley was a Federal Prosecutor with clearance to work in any State. He was thirty-eight and already making one hell of a name for himself in getting convictions on some of the most high-profile cases of the decade. That's who everyone saw him as, but to me, he was just *Noah.*

My big brother.

No one knew that I had any family and I kept it that way on purpose. I didn't want anyone targeting him to try and get to me. I had enemies; it was common practice when you killed as many high value targets as I had. When you had eliminated cartel leaders, mafia leaders, terrorists, and dirty politicians, the hard earned reputation was bound to rack up some enemies. It was why I didn't use a last name; it was why I didn't go by my legal name at all. The only one who knew my actual name was Noah and he never even called me it. He knew how dangerous my job was and the best thing about him, he never tried to pressure me into doing something different. He never tried to pressure me, period. He knew something horrible had happened to me growing up, something that permanently changed who I am, but he never pushed for answers. He allowed me to go at my own pace and I couldn't possibly love him more for it.

We were technically half-brothers. We had different mothers. Our father was a sorry excuse of a human being. Noah's mother refused to allow him in his life, whereas mine had hoped he would be this amazing man. In fairness to her, though, she was addicted to heroin so she could make herself believe she was a unicorn some days.

I had met Noah for the first time when I was nineteen and he was twenty-seven, at our father's funeral. Neither of us wanted to be there, but it was the only form of closure we were going to get. I was shocked to discover I had a brother, even a half-brother, and so was Noah. He instantly wanted to know me and he picked up that I was uncertain, too. We took it slow and now, eleven years later, I couldn't imagine going through life without talking to him at least once a week. He was the only person I had ever been able to open up to and talk for hours with.

"Hey, Brother. How are ya?" Noah asked the second he answered the phone.

"Good. Working a case I'm hoping you'll be able to help me out with."

"I'll do what I can. What do you need?"

"I'm working a serial killer case with the victims all male between twelve and fourteen. We have six confirmed to have been adopted. I'm hoping you could find out if the other six were as well. And maybe help with unsealing the adoption files."

"You think they might have been targeted for being adopted. That would mean someone that handled the adoption paperwork or has access to it, now, could be the killer. Yeah, that works for a warrant. Shoot me off all of the names and I'll pull what I can. I'll get my hands on the adoption records and send them over to you. You should have them tomorrow morning."

"Thanks, that's going to be a huge help. Everything okay with you?"

I knew he had been working some pretty challenging cases in the past few months. He was burning the midnight oil, and for a man who enjoyed sleeping, I knew it was taking a toll on him.

"I'm good. I just wrapped up a case in court this morning. I will get what you need and then I am off for a week. So, let me know if you need any other warrants or anything to help with your case."

"Appreciate it. Next time I get some vacation days, I'll come up your way. You can introduce me to this new man of yours."

Noah had started to see someone new a few months back. They weren't anything serious, but I still liked to make sure they were good enough for him. He hadn't been very lucky in love.

"Sounds good. I guess we'll see, if he's still sticking around by then. And hey, maybe you'll have a boyfriend as well."

That was highly unlikely. I didn't trust anyone enough to date someone. I didn't even have sex. But that was a whole other nightmare. One I wasn't looking to get into, right now.

I had to focus on these kids.

"Maybe. I gotta get back. Thanks, Noah."

"Anytime, Brother. Be safe. I love you."

"Love you, too."

I ended the call and then made the trip back into the conference room. I could see everyone's eyes on me and they were all clearly very interested in how I was connected to a federal prosecutor. I wasn't about to tell them.

"My guy is on it. He'll have the adoption files over for the morning."

"Perfect. Then we will be able to confirm if all twelve were adopted and who could be connected to them. Knox, the Governor has informed me that in the next hour there is going to be a press conference held out front of the Agency. You are going to address the press about the serial killer. The Governor is pulling rank, he wants everyone to know about the killings and he wants everyone keeping their eyes on the kids in every neighborhood," Mason said.

"The Mayor isn't going to like that," Knox instantly said, and I had to fight not to roll my eyes.

He was always so straight laced and afraid to do anything that might piss someone in the chain of command off.

Who cares what the Mayor wanted?

These were kids we were talking about. Parents deserved to know what was going on out there. Not to mention the kids deserved to know to be vigilant and not trust a stranger.

"Governor outranks the Mayor. I want

the age mentioned to be between ten and sixteen. I know he's only killed between twelve and fourteen, but we don't know what he will do if he can't get the age that he wants. He might be willing to go lower or higher to satisfy his need. While you are working on a speech, the rest of us will be going through the files. Let's get everything up on the board. I want to know what their injuries were, let's see if there's a pattern. Coop, you trace the injuries and see if anyone else that was killed or kidnapped within our age parameters had that injury. He didn't just develop his method overnight. He had to have practiced and perfected it. Ry, check into what he might need to torture and hold his victims. Let's get a list going so we can start cross referencing names," Mason ordered.

I gave Mason a nod and then went and sat down with my laptop. We needed as many lists as we could get so we could start cross-referencing and circling any that kept popping up. It wasn't solid evidence, but if there was a name or two on multiple lists, they were someone we wanted to look into more and interrogate. Sometimes, in an investigation like this, all you had to go off of in the beginning were lists.

***

It was roughly an hour later when I stood off to the side downstairs. Knox was starting his press conference and my job was to make sure no one looked suspicious. So far, all I could see were reporters far too eager to hear what had been going on. They had all been under a gag order for so long they were practically drooling to get some intel.

They were vultures, every last one of them.

From my position, I could see everything and hear what Knox was saying. I didn't really pay attention to him, though. I had heard all about the case and I didn't need to actively listen to it again.

What I could tell, though, was he enjoyed being up there. He enjoyed talking into the cameras and answering all of the questions. It made him feel special and that was the dumbest thing I had ever heard of.

Who the hell cared what a bunch of strangers thought of you?

Press conferences and high profile cases were what Knox was all about.

Anything he could use to push his career forward. It wouldn't surprise me, at all, if he was planning on writing a book about the cases he'd worked on.

Don't get me wrong, I had nothing against ambition or making money, but to gloat about your accomplishments was petty to me. Cops and the like should show up and do their job because they believed the world was going to be a safer place if they did. They shouldn't be doing their job in the hope of getting a gold star and a promotion out of it. That didn't make a good person, and I doubted that Knox truly was a good person deep down. As far as I was concerned, it was all a show, just an act he put on to make himself feel better.

God, I couldn't stand him and I hoped I would be able to leave soon and get the hell away from him. He didn't belong there, and after three months of having no suspects or leads, he didn't belong on the case. Clearly, he wasn't capable of solving this one and it would have been better to have another profiler on the case.

My opinion wasn't going to matter, though.

So, all I could do was what was in my capabilities and solve this case. Then, Knox would be out of my life for good and that would be the sweetest reward I had ever received.

CHAPTER FIVE

Knox

THE PRESS CONFERENCE had gone as well as could be expected. The reporters were starving for more information. They had been sitting on these homicides for months now, completely unable to report on them. It also didn't take them very long to start asking about why the Mayor had issued gag orders on these murders.

I'd tiptoed around those questions to the best of my ability and instead, had them focus on the children. They were what mattered the most in this situation. I also knew we would be getting a flood of calls from the victims' loved ones very soon. All of them would be demanding to know why they hadn't been informed of this earlier. Why we had stayed quiet, even with the gag orders.

They would be furious, but I couldn't blame them for that. There was a very real possibility that some of their children might still be alive had the Mayor not issued the gag order and had reported this serial killer to the press. It was also possible it wouldn't have changed anything, but the unknown of the 'what ifs' the parents were going to put themselves through would be devastating.

I hated that I hadn't been able to be honest with the victims' loved ones from the very beginning. I didn't like to lie and I hated not being able to give a parent all of the information they needed to understand what happened to their child.

Why their child had been killed.

It didn't matter how old a child was, they were always going to be their parents' baby. They were always going to be that sweet little child they brought home from the hospital, even if they were fifty at the time of their death. It was even hard to lie to the parents when it was something like this. When their child had been killed only because a serial killer had decided to make them his next victim.

There wasn't anything I could say to them to help them understand why this man was killing children. I could give them the profile and explain that, psychologically, he was born broken, but that wouldn't help them understand.

Because there simply was no understanding something like this.

Not when it was your child you had to bury.

I did mean every single word that I said about finding this sick bastard and putting him right where he belonged. An eight by ten hole in the ground where he would never see the light of day again.

We had been working away for a few hours, trying to combine lists and compare them. We had a lot of potential suspects, too many at this point. In a town like this, there were too many criminals; too many whack jobs that lived off the grid in a place where no one would hear someone scream.

I couldn't even be certain that our UnSub would even have a criminal record. Yes, he would likely have past offenses with either killing animals, or assaults, or starting fires, but it all depended on his family life growing up. Most parents didn't report their own children to the police. And if he came from a wealthy family, they could have easily paid the victims to cover it all up. He might not be in the system, which made everything we were doing even harder.

"Why no rape?" Ryzen asked, snapping the silence out of the room.

"What?" Rafe asked, obviously as confused as the rest of us.

I had to give it to Ryzen. When he decided to talk, he usually got everyone's attention. Though, that was mostly because he said something that confused everyone in the room as to what the hell he was even talking about. It would help if the man could speak full sentences.

"The UnSub. He goes through the trouble of kidnapping, torturing, and then killing, all without leaving a trace of himself on the bodies or at the kidnapping or dumping site. Why no sex?" Ryzen expanded.

I had to admit that was close to the most words I had ever heard him speak before.

"That *is* weird. He holds them for seventy-two hours and there's no indication that he touched them sexually, either with himself or an object," Mason said, understanding where Ryzen was going with this.

"Not every serial killer is a sexual sadist. A good number of serial killers torture and kill because it makes them feel good. Torture is foreplay to them, something they do that gets them off. They then fantasize about it later when they are masturbating. Now, if there had been signs of sexual trauma from an object, that would have meant that our UnSub isn't able to physically perform. But that's not the case here. Sex isn't something our UnSub wants with his victims. It's more about him satisfying his urge, his craving, to hurt and kill. He's a sadist. He gets off on the pain his victims are going through, but he's using that to pleasure himself afterward. He might even masturbate in the room with the boys just to see the fear in their eyes," I explained.

"All of the boys were naked for their

captivity, based on the injuries not having any clothing fibers in them. If he gets off on fear, there's nothing that scares a young teenage boy more than the fear of being raped," Ryzen said.

It wasn't necessarily the words that he used, but the tiniest hint of emotion that laced his voice that had me wondering. It almost sounded like he was speaking from experience and that piqued my interest.

When I had been evaluating Ryzen, it wasn't my original intention to have him fired. All I had was a file and most of it was redacted. My job was to make sure he could handle killing, essentially. He was a Government trained assassin and that took a mental toll on a person, especially when said person had been doing it for their entire adult life. At the age of eighteen, your mind is still developing, you are still learning not only who you are, but right and wrong. Physically, your mind isn't capable of processing killing other people in a healthy manner. Medically, it's not possible. That was why so many young adults had a hard time when they were in the military. They go off to war at the young age of eighteen or nineteen and see the horrors that war has to offer. They then can't deal with what they have seen or done, so they turn to drinking and drugs. They develop PTSD, and then it's a straight shot down from there.

For Ryzen, I wanted to make sure he was handling the killing. I wanted to make sure it would be safe for him to keep killing. However, his attitude and his lack of words at the time told me he couldn't be killing. It told me that his view of the world had become too dark for him to know the difference between right and wrong. But I had wondered if that view had been skewed before he even arrived at the CIA.

Hearing him speaking like this, it only made me wonder if my initial thoughts were correct. That the world had been dark for him long before he even stepped foot in the CIA. If that was true, though, that opened my mind up to all sorts of questions, and especially, one of the more pressing questions.

Was he picked up by the CIA for another reason?

"This UnSub would probably get off on seeing the fear. He might have even given his victims the choice of being hurt or raped. It's quite possible they picked being tortured over being raped. Unfortunately, unless we can get the UnSub to talk, we might never know exactly what he has done to them," I stated.

"There doesn't seem to be a pattern in the torture. One victim he electrocutes, another he burns, another he cuts. It's all random and each one has some that are similar, but they also have something new each time," Roland said as he flipped through the photos.

"He could still be perfecting his method," Jarod supplied.

"Most likely, he hasn't discovered what will bring him the greatest pleasure, yet. Serial killers are just like heroin addicts. The first time they kill, it's messy and unorganized but it feels amazing. Most have been dreaming, fantasizing about killing someone for years. It's built up inside of them and when they get to experience it the first time, it's orgasmic to them. However, just like a heroin addict, they have to keep chasing that first time experience. Each kill doesn't give them the same high that their first kill did. So, they have to do it more often and they have to do more to their victims to get that same first time feeling. It's why each victim has more torture done to them. He's trying to figure out what will give him that level of satisfaction that his first kill did," I explained.

"Does it work in our favor that he is still learning?" Rafe asked.

"It could. He's still learning what works for him, so he's inexperienced and that can lead to him making a mistake. I suspect that he's younger as well. In his mid-twenties to mid-thirties. He's not impulsive, because he can wait a week in between victims. He has to be relatively physically fit to be able to carry dead weight of up to eighty pounds, too," I answered.

"He's not leaving behind any fingerprints or hair, so either he's bald and wearing gloves, or he's covered when he tortures and dumps them," Cooper said.

"That seems smart for a newbie," Ryzen commented.

"That's the thing, there's no short supply of serial killer books. During his fantasy stages, he could have easily been doing research on best practices. On how to kidnap and dump a body. Studying how law enforcement caught other serial killers and learning from their mistakes.

The Internet and science helps us catch them, but it also helps them evade capture. It's a double-edged sword," I stated.

"He hasn't perfected his method yet, so he has to be new. Coop, did you get anything from past police reports on animal cruelty?" Mason asked.

"A very long list. Even after I eliminated any females and recent reports."

"Any name pop up more than once?" Hollingsworth asked.

"A bunch. People are really screwed up in this town."

"There's more black magic and witchcraft in this state than anywhere else in the country. A lot of those animal cruelty charges will be connected to black magic, sometimes they sacrifice an animal for their rituals, or rooster fighting. There's a large underground cock fighting group here. In the reports, though, it will specify what they were for. If you add black magic and rooster fighting to the filters, it will eliminate them and give us a better picture of what we're dealing with."

"I'll do that now," Cooper said as he turned his attention to his computer.

"Well, given the black magic angle, could this be ritual?" Roland asked.

I had wondered that myself when the first victim appeared. It wouldn't be the first time someone was killing a person and offering them up as a human sacrifice. However, the second victim told me that wasn't what was going on.

"Human sacrifices are usually drained of their blood as part of the offering. They also have symbols painted or carved into their body. They don't get tortured, because it can ruin the offering. They all die from exsanguination. They are placed within a pentagram and they are bled until they stop breathing. It's a long death, but a relatively painless one," I explained.

"Definitely not what this guy is doing," Hollingsworth said.

Mason's phone rang and he pulled it out to answer. He moved outside to speak with whoever was on the other end. I hoped it was some good news for us. That whoever was calling would be able to give us a clue as to who this UnSub was. The call didn't last very long, and Mason strolled back into the room. Based on the look on his face, he wasn't happy with whatever intel he just received.

"Calls are coming in on the tip line.

Most of them are people asking for more information. However, there was a series of calls that had been placed using a burner phone and a voice modulator. The man claimed to be the UnSub and he has been calling threatening to kill Special Agent Knox Hunter."

"He's just posturing. I don't fit his victimology. Assuming he even is our UnSub."

I knew that some serial killers would reach out to the media. I had gone through this before when they weren't happy that the Feds were investigating them. They wanted fame and glory and killing was how they were going about getting it. But this time around, we had no reason to believe it was the UnSub and even if it was, I wasn't a twelve to fourteen year old boy. He wasn't going to come after me. He didn't have the courage to.

"Regardless, your boss is not looking to take any chances. He is ordering you to be placed in protective custody until this UnSub has been caught. And I agree. There's no point in taking the risk of you being grabbed. When killers have been backed into a corner, they lash out at anyone. If he believes the investigation into him dies with you, he won't think twice about killing you," Mason stated.

I knew there was no way I was going to get out of this.

I didn't need to be in protective custody. I highly doubted this UnSub would come for me. Even if he thought he could keep killing by killing me. I was a lot bigger than he was used to grabbing. Plus, I was a high profile Profiler. Grabbing me would mean the full force of the FBI would come down on him. It was essentially suicide. He had been smart this whole time. He wasn't going to make that fatal mistake.

"Fine, I will go to a safe house every night," I conceded.

"And that would usually be perfectly acceptable. However, your boss also informed me that you don't always do as you are told when you get a lead on a case. That you have gone out into the field before without backup because you figured something out. Because of that, you are going to be staying with one of us to ensure you don't leave on your own."

This was ridiculous.

The few times I had gone out on my own it was perfectly safe. I didn't go to a killer's house or some deserted area of the city. I went to populated areas to chase down a lead. Nothing ever happened to me. Now, I was being stuck with a babysitter again and I didn't appreciate it.

"Who gets him?" Rafe asked.

"Well, only two of you have the safest homes on the team. But I am not going to place him with you, Rafe, because I'm not going to put Lilly at risk. Not with a serial killer targeting children," Mason started, but Ryzen cut him off.

"No."

"You have the safest house," Mason started.

Oh hell, no.

I was with Ryzen on this one. I would rather be captured by this UnSub then trapped in a house with Rumpelstiltskin. It also didn't surprise me that his house would be one of the safest. He probably had ten guns in each room and a bomb that would go off if you stepped on the welcome mat the wrong way.

"He's not living with me," Ryzen pressed.

"He is, because I'm ordering it. We have to keep him alive. The safest place for him to be is your house. If you don't want your house being used as a safe house, don't turn the thing into Fort Knox. It's been a long day. I suggest everyone go home, get some sleep, and then we can start fresh tomorrow morning. We will have the court files by then and, hopefully, that will shed some light for us," Mason said, his tone firm and final.

I knew there was no arguing against him on this. I was rooming with Ryzen, whether I liked it or not.

He would probably murder me in my

sleep.

CHAPTER SIX

Ryzen

THIS FUCKING SUCKED.

The very last person I wanted anywhere near my home was Knox. I didn't make my home secure so it could be used as a safe house for any stray that came along. It was designed this way to ensure I would be safe while inside. To ensure that none of my enemies would be able to get to me as long as I was in my home. So I could sleep at night and not have to be on edge waiting for an attack.

There were people out there that would love to get their hands on me. Either to kill me or to try and get me to turn against my country and be a sniper for them. I didn't survive the shit I did growing up just to be captured as an adult. Not while I was old enough and strong enough to defend myself. The reality that I lived in was the fact that I would always have enemies. It was part of the reason why I never dated anyone. They didn't need a target on their back.

Besides, dating was overrated.

There was no point to it. It was just another social convention that made no sense and was completely useless. If the world needed to increase in population, which it didn't, people could just have sex and make a baby. They didn't need to date to have sex.

Sex was also overrated.

Everything involving sex was overrated. From kissing to the actual deed. There was no point in any of it, at least not to me. It also hurt and anyone that said sex didn't hurt had clearly never been a bottom. There was nothing pleasant about the experience and it only left me feeling empty. I never got off on it. I'd never had a guy make me come. Fuck, I almost never got hard when someone touched me. Sex was animalistic and should only be done when the need to increase the population called for it.

If that meant you never had sex because you were gay, then so what?

It wasn't like a person needed sex to

survive. You didn't need an orgasm to keep living and even if you did, that's what your hand was for. I was done with sex. I was done with all of it a long time ago.

There was nothing I could do or say to make Mason change his mind about Knox coming to stay with me. As much as I would have liked for him to stay with Rafe, I also understood why that was a terrible idea. There was no way any of us were going to risk Lilly. We knew Fin would be fine to take care of himself, but Lilly had already been through so much, we weren't going to risk putting her through anything else.

I didn't say anything. I just got up and strolled out the door. If Knox was going to be staying with me, then he could follow or not, the choice was up to him.

Personally, I didn't give two shits if the UnSub grabbed him or not. I could hear him following me, though, so apparently, he cared. We got into my car once again and he spoke.

"I need to pick up some clothes at my place."

"Address?"

"1033 Parkview Ave."

I started my car and headed for his address. The sooner we solved this case, the better off I was going to be. We drove in silence for a good ten minutes before he felt the need to break it. I don't know why.

"Who is Lilly?"

"What?"

"Lilly. Mason said I couldn't be with Rafe because of Lilly. I was just curious who she was."

It wasn't any of his business who Lilly was or anything about our personal lives. At the same time, though, it wasn't like Rafe or any of the other guys wouldn't share the information with him. I could refuse to answer the question, tell him to mind his own business, but that was going to put him in a sour mood and I was going to be stuck in my house for the next twelve hours with him.

"It's a bit of a story. Basically, Rafe went undercover with his boyfriend, Finley, into a human trafficking ring. Lilly is Fin's six year old niece, almost seven, now. Fin's older brother and his wife were killed so the trafficking ring could take Lilly. Fin worked undercover for nineteen months, eighteen alone and one with Rafe, before we found Lilly and shut it down. They all live together, now."

"My God. That poor girl. Is she healing okay?"

There was genuine concern to his voice and that surprised me. I didn't think he was capable of caring about anyone. He always seemed to be more interested in reading the paperwork than actually getting to know someone without judgment first.

"She has her dads, she'll be fine. She's in personal therapy and group therapy. She stays home from school, for now, but they live in a gated community with good security. She's safe. They've been thinking about a service dog for her. I guess the nightmares are bad."

I knew what it felt like to have night terrors. I knew what it felt like to be scared to close your eyes, to dread what you'd see. I still had that issue. All too often, I'd stay awake for a few days before going to sleep. My insomnia was always on, no matter what I did. It wasn't easy for me to just fall asleep. Not after all of the horrors I had lived through. The horrors I had seen. Despite what everyone chose to believe, despite what Knox thought he knew about me, the killing did bother me. I was taking a life and it didn't matter if the person was a criminal or not, I was still collecting souls and I had a lot of them. Close to a thousand now, between growing up and the CIA. It was a lot of souls to carry around and they did get very heavy.

I kept doing it, though, and not because I was gifted with a gun, but because these people needed to be taken out. They were too dangerous to keep alive. Not killing them meant thousands more would die and that wasn't something I could live with. It was just better to kill them and carry around their soul, compared to thousands of other innocent people that I refused to protect because I refused to pull the trigger.

It was a lot to try and live with and I wasn't certain I had figured out the balance for it, yet. I was trying. I was trying to sleep and have more of a normal life, but it wasn't working so far.

When Mason had reached out looking for help on the Task Force, I had thought about saying no. I had never worked within a team before. The CIA always worked alone, and even if they didn't, as a sniper, I sure as shit did. Growing up, I was always on my own so there was no team playing there. I wasn't really sure how to operate on a team or if I even wanted to be on one. Still, I didn't have anything else going on and it was a chance to take down a corrupt cop. When it was over, I was ready to leave, but then Mason had said we could stay and keep working the Task Force. It seemed like the right thing to do.

I had never wanted siblings. I had never wanted brothers. I never felt like I needed anyone in my life, but working alongside the guys, it was different. It made me feel different. The hole that had always been inside of me wasn't so big anymore. It was still there, but it wasn't as big and I didn't feel so empty. Working for the Agency, with the guys, it all felt right and I was glad that I had taken Mason up on his offer. I was glad that Mason had called me when most probably wouldn't have.

"A service dog will help with the nightmares. And a weighted blanket can do wonders for insomnia and anxiety. That might be something they consider as well. Unfortunately, all they can really do is keep her in therapy and wait it out. The good news is that she is young enough her mind will bounce back. She'll be able to have a normal life without the trauma destroying her."

Hopefully, that was true, but I knew from personal experience the things you saw at Lilly's age could haunt you for the rest of your life. As for the weighted blanket, I knew they worked. I had one permanently on my bed to try and help me at night. On the nights I could bring myself to close my eyes, it helped with the nightmares and anxiety about sleeping. I was hoping that Lilly would recover better than I did and she would be able to be happy and healthy. She had two great dads in her life, though, so I was sure she would.

After a quick stop at Knox's place and a pizza joint, we arrived at my house. The house wasn't in the outskirts, but I wasn't right in the middle of town, either. There was a metal, electrified fence all around my property. My closest neighbor was half a block away. I had an alarm on both the front and back doors, along with every window in the house. It was a two-story house with a fully completed basement. I had that set up as a gym with my treadmill and my weight set. It was a nice house. It was small and that was how I liked it. I didn't want too big of a house, there were too many spaces someone could hide and it would be too much work to clean.

We climbed out of my car and I strode over to unlock my door with my keycode. I didn't do keys, too easy to copy, but having a lock with a passcode meant someone would need my fourteen digit code to unlock the door. And then, they would need my iris scan to shut my alarm off. I knew Knox was going to have some comment about the high level of security, but if it helped me to sleep, if it helped me to feel safe in my own home, it was worth it to me.

"I guess Mason wasn't kidding with the Fort Knox joke," Knox commented as he stepped inside behind me and closed the door.

"When you've made a living taking out some of the worst criminals in this world, it's vital to have a strong security system,"

I said as I brought the pizza into the kitchen and slid it onto the counter.

"Fair enough," Knox said, and I could tell he was already looking around and trying to analyze everything. It was just another reason why I didn't want him in my home. I didn't need a Profiler psychoanalyzing me.

I turned the lights on in the kitchen and spoke.

"I don't have a spare room, so you'll have to sleep on the couch. I'll bring you down a pillow and blanket."

I didn't wait to hear any comments from him. I went upstairs and quickly grabbed him a pillow and spare blanket before I went back down and dropped them on the couch.

Knox was still standing in the kitchen and I could tell he wanted to go and explore the house. I just grabbed a plate with some pizza and a water bottle from the fridge before I headed back upstairs, leaving him to do whatever he wanted to do. I wasn't dealing with him tonight. I had done my job. I got him here and he was still alive. It was on him to entertain himself. I was certain he would be able to do that easily enough with profiling my home. I was sure, come morning, I would hear all about how my home told him I was a whack job who needed to find a different career. That would only give him more ammo, only give him more confidence in his decision to end my career with the CIA.

Well, he could entertain himself in his perfect black and white world. I would be too busy trying to fall asleep tonight. I hadn't gotten any sleep in the past two days and I really needed to try and catch a few hours tonight. Though, with having someone in my home, chances were I would be spending the night staring up at the ceiling and waiting for the sun to rise.

CHAPTER SEVEN

Knox

THE SECOND I heard Ryzen's bedroom door close, I couldn't help but look around. I couldn't believe the security he had for his house. At first, I thought he was being paranoid. That wouldn't really be too uncommon with snipers. They were always hyper-vigilant and believed that someone was always watching them. But hearing that he had dangerous enemies out there, that did make a lot more sense. It made sense that he would have this level of security on his home.

I didn't know what type of targets he had killed, but I did know that the CIA took out major terrorists, cartels, the mafia, and high-powered weapon traffickers. There were an endless number of criminals out there who would want to take revenge on someone like Ryzen. I wasn't going to hold the security measures against him.

I moved into the living room and turned on the lights. I noticed right away that the lights weren't very bright. Even in the kitchen they were dim. I'd thought at first that maybe the bulbs were starting to burn out, but when the living room was just the same it just made me more curious. Plus, the curtains were blackout curtains and they were pulled closed. It was definitely weird. But maybe with being a sniper, he was worried about someone looking in. That hyper-vigilance again, I guess. Shrugging, I continued my perusal.

The furniture in the room was basic and looked either secondhand or like he'd had them for a good five or so years. There was a black suede couch, a black leather chair, and a matching recliner. Other than the furniture, there was a coffee table and two end tables that were brown, and a flat screen TV that sat perched on a brown entertainment stand on the opposite wall from the furniture, and that was it. There was nothing else in the room at all.

Hell, there was nothing else on this

whole floor.

Not even a kitchen table.

There was nothing personal in the whole main level of the house. Nothing on the walls, not even any of those scenescape type photos that you could pick up in a store. The walls were completely bare. No family photos, though that could be blamed on him not wanting any enemies to know anything personal about him. But he could at least have a photo of a sunset or something. It didn't have to be anything with family in it, but something that reflected who he was. Something, *anything* that made the place feel like a home and not just a rest stop.

I shook my head and then made my way into the kitchen and opened the cupboards to see what he had. There were only a handful of plates and bowls, and two mugs. That was it for dishes. In the other cupboard, there was instant powdered coffee—*nasty*—and a stockpile of military MRE food. Why the hell he wanted to eat that crap I had no idea. I could understand the need while he was working in a remote area for the CIA, but he wasn't a sniper anymore. He could cook food while working for the Agency.

I moved over to the fridge and saw that he only had milk in the whole thing. Checking the freezer next showed me the single portion, microwavable meals. For a man who was highly trained in hand to hand combat and shooting, I would've thought he'd eat better. Though, now that I thought about it, maybe with him working for the CIA since he was eighteen, he didn't actually know how to cook. If he had been working a lot of hours and always traveling, learning how to cook wouldn't be high on his priority list.

I was going to assume that if I gave him a cookbook, he wouldn't take too kindly to it.

I closed the freezer and grabbed a plate, sliding a couple slices of pizza on it and balancing it in one hand before I grabbed my laptop with the other and strolled over to the couch. I had some work I could do on this case and, eventually, I would get some sleep. Hopefully, tomorrow we would be able to find our connection through the adoption files and stop this UnSub before they grabbed another kid.

CHAPTER EIGHT

Knox

IT WAS JUST after seven in the morning when I finally woke up. I had drifted off to sleep around midnight, give or take, so I had a good seven hours under my belt.

I stretched and then sat up. The couch was surprisingly comfortable and I could understand why Ryzen would have kept it around. I was a man who loved function, so if the couch was comfortable, I was all for it. Same as a bed. There were two things that I needed to be comfortable in my life, my couch and my bed.

I climbed to my feet and decided it would be safe to open the curtains and let some of the sunlight shine in. The sun was already coming up and it instantly brightened up the room. I was about to make my way into the kitchen when I heard Ryzen coming down the stairs. Apparently, he was an early riser as well.

He let out a groan as he covered his eyes and spoke. "Fuck, close the curtains."

I had no idea what was going on, but I instantly yanked them shut, blocking out the bright rays that had been beaming into the room moments before. He wasn't wearing his sunglasses. I spoke as I walked over to him.

"Sorry, I didn't think it would be a problem to open the curtains."

"It's fine," he said, and for the first time I could see his actual eyes.

They were grey.

They were beautiful.

That thought surprised me, because I had never found another man's eyes to be beautiful before. I was straight, always had been, but *beautiful* was the only word I could think of to describe them.

"You have grey eyes. That's why you have the blackout curtains and always wear sunglasses, why the lights are so dim," I said with complete understanding.

"And you figured it was because I was paranoid and an asshole," he said as he went to grab the instant coffee.

His statement was fair, because that

was exactly what I thought. I might be overanalyzing him and that wasn't fair to him.

"I'm sorry. I get too comfortable with being a Profiler that sometimes I forget that not everyone fits into a box perfectly. Look, to clear the air between us, I didn't know the CIA would fire you. I thought they would put you into a different position. You'd been a sniper for them for close to ten years. That's a very long time with a very large kill count. Psychologically, it's not good for you to keep being a sniper that long."

I knew there was a massive elephant in the room between us and it would be better to clear the air so we could work with each other without all of this hostility between us. It was great to hope that we would catch this UnSub within the next forty-eight hours, but the odds weren't in our favor. It would be nice to be able to work beside him without feeling like nails were going through my skin.

"I know how to handle my job. It wasn't your place to tell me or anyone when to stop. I didn't become a black hat sniper like you claimed I would. I still work for the good guys."

"Part of my job as a Profiler is to give those evaluations and decide if someone is mentally able to handle the work, still. I honestly thought it would be better for you, Ry, to not be a sniper with the CIA. But like I said, I thought they would put you in a different position. I'm sorry if you felt like I made the wrong call or like my decision was an attack against you. I was just doing my job, that was all."

"Sure. We should head out soon. If you

want to shower, bathroom is the door on the left."

He wasn't going to talk to me about it, that much was clear. The situation and my responsibility in it, wasn't something we were going to see eye to eye on. There wasn't a point in me trying to get him to understand, we were too different, but hopefully now, we could at least get along a bit better if he were willing to consider that I didn't have it out for him.

Maybe.

I went and grabbed my bag so I could take a shower and get changed. I decided I would wear jeans today. Everyone else in the Agency wore jeans and not dress clothes, so I figured it would be better to blend in with them.

I jogged up the stairs and the first room I walked by was his bedroom. The door was open and I couldn't help but to go inside. The same type of blackout curtains covered the windows, leaving the room dark. I now knew it wasn't paranoia. I flipped on the light and moved further inside. The black blanket on his bed had me going over to it. I picked it up and confirmed exactly what I thought.

It was a weighted blanket.

The most common reason someone used a weighted blanket was anxiety. I had suspected that the killing didn't bother Ryzen, and that was one of my main concerns and why I suggested he stop being a sniper, but maybe I was wrong about that. Maybe Ryzen had just gotten very good at hiding his anxiety and emotions. This room also had nothing personal in it. I couldn't help but wonder if maybe Ryzen didn't know how to have a home, so he didn't know how to make it into one, either.

Crap, now I had even more questions about him and I'd thought I was done with questions for him. I thought I had already figured him out and now, it looked like I truly didn't know anything about the man, after all.

CHAPTER NINE

Knox

"WHAT ABOUT A woman UnSub?" Ryzen asked, breaking the silence.

For the past few hours, we had all been combing through the adoption files that Ryzen's friend had managed to get for us. As it turned out, all twelve victims had been adopted, and most of them were closed adoptions. It gave us a huge suspect pool, but it was a start and it was something we were diving headfirst into.

"Out of all serial killers in the United States, only approximately eleven percent are females. Female serial killers are very rarely sadistic. They tend to kidnap children because they feel like they need to be rescued. They take care of them and they die because they failed to properly feed or give them water. It's not because they physically killed them. Any female serial killers who were sadistic, they targeted males or females who they felt did them wrong in some way. It could be as simple as a woman accidentally bumping into her man. The killer will kidnap that woman and torture her to death while justifying her actions because that victim must have been trying to steal her man. They never go for children to hurt," I explained.

If the victims hadn't been tortured, I would be thinking our perp was a female as well. It would explain how the victims were lured, since most children will trust a female over a male. When a child is abducted, people are looking at the men in the area as potential suspects and they ignore the women. But with the psychopathy of this UnSub, it just wasn't possible.

"So we can eliminate the women on the lists," Cooper said, nodding as he got to work on eliminating potential suspects.

"Anyone over the age of forty, to be safe, and younger than twenty," I added.

"I would imagine they can't be well known, either. If a judge was walking down the street and grabbed a kid, someone would notice," Mason pointed out.

"Correct. Anyone who had been in the news as often as judges are would have been noticed. We can also eliminate anyone who has been out of the state during the past three months, and anyone who has been arrested or in the hospital. Our UnSub was able to stalk all of his victims for at least a week. That takes time and dedication," I said.

"Anyone check parking tickets?" Ryzen asked.

"From the courthouse?" Jarod asked, confused.

"Outside of the victim's home, and at the kidnapping or dumping site. The UnSub stalked them, so maybe he got a ticket while he was following them on foot," Ryzen explained.

"That's smart. He might not have paid

attention to the parking bylaws if he was fixated on his victim. Each parking ticket is recorded into the system with the license plate and location. Can you run them?" I asked Cooper.

I hadn't even thought about looking for parking tickets. I was so focused on finding our UnSub that I didn't think to try and find his car. If we could find the car, we might be able to track it back to an address or a neighborhood, at least.

"I can run them. It'll be a lot, though, but I can cross reference them with the locations and record the path the victims took around their kidnapping," Cooper said.

I knew it wasn't going to be that simple for him. It wasn't like we had a make or a model for the car. We didn't have anything he could truly use to do a targeted search, but he might be able to narrow it down enough that we could compare it to our long list of suspects. We didn't have much, but I felt like we were at least getting somewhere.

For the first time in three months, I was getting somewhere.

CHAPTER TEN

Knox

AT TWO IN the morning, you would think I would be asleep. Instead, I couldn't get my mind off of the case. I couldn't stop thinking about it. We had been able to accomplish a lot and still nothing all at the same time today. We had a very long list of suspects, even after all of the refining we had managed to do. We had a lot that we could be looking at and yet, at the same time, we had nothing more than we did yesterday. It was frustrating, but at least there hadn't been another child taken, yet. Not that I expected there to be. We still had five days before he would strike out again.

I noticed a shadow coming down the stairs and glanced over to see that Ryzen was still awake, too. He walked into the kitchen and I figured he was grabbing a glass of water.

I pushed the blanket off of me and made my way into the kitchen. Ryzen had no shirt on and was just wearing sleep pants. Even in the dimly lit room, from the light that I had left on, I could see the scars covering his back.

I can't even explain what happened at that moment, what made me respond the way I did. It was like a magnet had been attached to the both of us and I was suddenly being pulled to him. Before I could even register what I was doing, my hand lightly ghosted along the one scar on his back. The whisper of the touch had him tensing, but he didn't pull away.

I knew what this scar was.

It was long, but not jagged. I had seen these type of scars from photos during my training days at Quantico.

Ryzen had been whipped.

Someone had actually taken a whip to his back; not once, but fifteen times. His back was covered in them, along with other smaller scars.

Someone had done this to him.

Someone had tortured him.

I felt my breath hitch and my fingers tingled as I traced each scar. My heart ached for what the man must have gone through, how this torture must have felt.

The scars were old. This horrible torment had to be done to him close to a dozen years ago.

All before he was eighteen.

Christ, he'd been just a child.

My mind played his words over again in my head. The words he spoke about the fear of being raped to keep a child in line. My stomach turned at knowing that he must have been speaking from personal experience. Anger grew in the pit of my stomach and bile rose up my throat. I had never truly felt this angry before, but I wanted nothing more than to go and find the person responsible for these scars and kill the fucker with my own bare hands. To do this to someone, to do this to a child, it was disgusting, and it only painted a clearer picture as to why Ryzen was the way he was.

He wasn't a killer.

He was a fucking warrior and I had completely misjudged him.

"Who did this to you?" I growled out as I fought to control my rage.

CHAPTER ELEVEN

Ryzen

I HADN'T REALIZED Knox was awake. I had been in my room, laying in my bed and trying to get myself to close my eyes, but no matter what I did, I just couldn't do it. I was so tired, completely drained, mentally and physically, but I couldn't sleep.

Insomnia was a cruel bitch.

I figured I would come down and grab a glass of water and maybe go for a run on my treadmill to try and wear myself out even more. I was so used to being alone in my house that, in my exhausted state, I didn't even remember Knox was down here until I saw him lying on the couch.

I heard him coming over to me and I was hoping he was just going to comment that he couldn't sleep, either. I wasn't expecting him to touch me. I wasn't expecting the anger in his voice at the sight of my scars.

I had made peace with my scars a long time ago. They weren't something I felt I needed to hide away from the world. I had, in the beginning, tried to ignore them, pretended like they weren't there. But every time I removed my shirt, I was reminded of them. It was unavoidable. There was nothing I could do to cover them up. I had even entertained the idea of getting tattoos to cover them, but there were far too many to cover and I really didn't like needles, which would be a hiccup for getting a tattoo.

In the handful of times, I had been with someone sexually since I was eighteen, the person was always freaked out by them. They didn't like touching them, they didn't like seeing them and always had me hide them while we were having sex. For a long time, they made me feel like I was worthless and disgusting.

Disfigured.

Noah was the one to help me understand and see that they weren't a sign of weakness. They weren't something that I should have to hide away like a dirty secret. They were proof of how strong I was. They were proof that I was a fighter and any guy that didn't understand that could go fuck themselves.

I was comfortable with them being seen, but that didn't mean I wanted to openly talk about them. Especially with a man like Knox. I couldn't tell if he was asking me about them because he genuinely wanted to know, or because his Profiler's mind was working overtime at seeing them. I could hear the anger in his voice, but that didn't mean he wasn't examining me in a Profiler way. There were plenty of Profilers that I'd come across in my time with the CIA that could get angry and upset at the sight of a hurt victim, but that didn't change that they were still analyzing their every move. I wasn't looking to be analyzed or dissected.

"I don't need an e-val," I stated.

"No, that's not why I was asking. I was asking because I would like to get my hands on the asshole who did this to you. Put him in a dark hole for the rest of his fucking life," Knox said as his voice shook with anger.

His fury truly did surprise me, because I wasn't expecting it. It was no secret that we didn't start off on the best foot. We didn't like each other. We were polar opposites. I doubted he had experienced anything horrible in his life. I doubted he had ever gotten his heart broken. I knew his parents raised him right and he went to Harvard for his degree. A degree he proudly framed and hung in his office for everyone to see.

I had never even been to high school. I hadn't even been to grade school. I spoke English, not always that well, and a few African dialects that I'd picked up in order to survive. I had never been referred to as the brains. I was always the muscle, always the shooter, and that was perfectly fine with me. I was damn good at shooting. I had been taught from a very young age how to do it. Knox barely knew how to hold a gun.

He didn't care about me, so why the hell would he care about getting his hands on the person who did this to me?

"Why do you care?"

The question probably didn't matter and I doubted I could believe what he said, but I still found myself needing to ask it. I needed to know why he would care so much about who had hurt me.

"Because you didn't deserve to have any of this done to you. Because I can tell they are from your childhood. Whoever did this to you is a monster and they deserve to be punished. Mostly, though, because I judged you when I shouldn't have. I don't tend to get my perspective on people wrong, but with you, Ry, I admit, I got it very wrong. I thought the killing didn't bother you. That you had shut down emotionally and socially. That was why you didn't talk and why you acted as if you didn't care. But you *do* care. You haven't slept in days. I can see it in the way your movements are getting a bit slower. I saw the weighted blanket on your bed, telling me you have anxiety. You don't have it during the day, though, I haven't seen any signs, so it's just around sleeping. Nightmares, would be my guess. These scars, they tell me that you are a survivor. They tell me that you are a warrior and you became a sniper not just because you were good at it, but because you wanted to protect people. You wanted to make the world safer for children. And you quietly pay the price for it without complaint."

Fuck.

I wasn't really sure what to do with that. It would have been a lot easier if Knox had just stayed the cold-hearted, single-minded asshole that he was that day five years ago in his office. It would have made things a lot easier to handle, to deal with, if he had. This wasn't something that I talked about, because the scars didn't come from a single person. There wasn't one person who could take the blame for every mark on me. There was one person who started the chain of events, but he was already dead. There was no one to go and arrest. There was no one to put into the ground. They were already dead and not by my own hands. It should have brought me some semblance of peace knowing that they were dead and they couldn't hurt me or another child ever again, but it didn't. I knew there was someone else taking their place and keeping the practice going. There would always be someone else to take up the mantle and keep hurting children. It was an endless merry-go-round and it wasn't going to stop. At least, not in my lifetime.

"The people responsible are already dead and no, it wasn't by me."

"Good. They're in Hell where they belong. Can you tell me who they were?"

he asked, cautiously.

Clearly, he didn't want to cross the line or push when he shouldn't. I could tell he wasn't too sure where the line was, though, and he was trying to see if it was okay for him to know more or if I needed him to stop. He was leaving the ball in my court and I greatly appreciated it.

I turned to face him as I spoke. "They weren't anyone special. My father wasn't a good man and my mother was a heroin addict. She overdosed when I was five and my father's idea of parenting was to send me to Africa to live within a missionary. They traveled around the war torn villages trying to help where they could."

"Did your father know that?" he asked, as his hand lightly traced a scar that went over my heart and down my left side.

"I don't think he cared enough to find

out. I was nine when the rebels attacked the camp the missionary was living in. They grabbed me and I was turned into a child soldier for them. I was with them until I was rescued roughly three years later by a mercenary who was a sniper. He taught me everything I know. For five years, we traveled all over the country taking out major threats against innocent people. CIA caught wind of me and the rest is history."

Being a child soldier hadn't been easy. There were plenty of moments in my life back then that made me want to give up. That made me want to conform to what they were demanding of me. Maybe it would have been easier to give in, to let my mind be conditioned into doing what they wanted. However, I didn't want to be a murderer. I didn't want to kill innocent people, other children, all because they didn't want to join an army. I knew I was a murderer, it was a fact that I'd had to deal with and I would have to continue to live with it for the rest of my life. I had killed innocent people, all before the age of puberty. I wasn't trying to focus on that. I was trying to focus on all of the lives I had saved by taking out dangerous targets. Maybe then, I could tip the scale in my favor.

"I'm so sorry. You should never have been put into that position. Your father never should have sent you there. That mercenary never should have turned you into a weapon and the CIA should never have recruited you. They should have freed you, not used you, too."

"I chose it. The CIA gave me a choice and I don't regret it. I've saved thousands of lives by the kills I've made. I'm well aware that, under different circumstances, I would be a serial killer, a mass murderer for all of the souls I've collected in my life. But every time I killed a target, I was saving thousands of innocent lives and that is always worth the price to my own soul."

I'm not sure when it happened, but the distance between us had become considerably smaller and not just in a physical sense. I shouldn't have told him any of this, but I wanted him to know. I wanted him to understand why I am the way that I am. That it wasn't for the reasons he'd suspected. That it wasn't for the reasons that he'd put in his report to the CIA. Yes, I was mad about losing my position in the Agency. However, if I had still been working for the CIA, I never would have been able to take Mason up on his offer to join his new Agency. As much as I wasn't certain at first, I didn't want to work for anyone else. I wanted to work for the Federal Protection Agency and keep helping children who believed no one was coming for them. Losing my position at the CIA might actually have been the best thing to ever happen to me, and I couldn't hate Knox for that.

Knox was so close to me, now, that I had to tilt my head back to be able to look him in the eyes. He was taller than me by six inches and, more often than not, I hated it when a man was this close to me, looking down at me. However, with Knox, I didn't feel like he was trying to intimidate me. There was an emotion in his eyes that I couldn't pinpoint. I had never seen it before, in anyone's eyes. It wasn't pity, hate, or disgust. It wasn't even sadness. I didn't know what it was, but it made me feel weird. Having him this close to me, his hand on my chest over my heart, it was all making me feel weird.

"You're a good man, Ry. You are sacrificing so much of yourself for people you don't even know. Not many men would be able to do that. You don't have to carry it alone, though. I'll always be there for you, should you need to talk or just don't want to be alone."

What was happening?

Why was he making me feel this way?

What the hell was this feeling, anyway?

I had been with a handful of guys since I was eighteen and I had never felt like this toward them. They had never made me feel like this. I didn't even know how to describe it. There was just this *warmth.* It was weird and I wasn't certain I liked it. He shouldn't be this close to me.

So why didn't I want him to move back?

Why couldn't I stop looking at his lips?

This was insane. I wasn't attracted to him. I *couldn't be* attracted to him. We were too different and one of those major differences was him being straight. I knew he was straight. I had seen the photos of him and a girlfriend in his office. Everything I'd heard about him through the grapevine was that he liked women. He had never been with a guy before.

But if he was only attracted to women, why was he standing so close to me?

Our bodies were touching, he had his hand on my chest, but his arm wasn't extended. We were touching fully. I could feel his stomach against mine. I could feel the silhouette of his dick through his sweatpants against my lower stomach and I knew he could feel mine on his upper thigh.

If he wasn't attracted to men, why could I feel him getting harder?

Why was he looking at me like this?

His hand traveled down from my chest and slowly moved down my left side and to my hip. My sweatpants sat low on my hips and his hand dipped under the elastic waistband to rest lower on my hip. I could see the heat in his eyes and it shocked me.

Knox wanted to kiss me.

I should pull away. I should push him away and put that wall back up between us.

This was so wrong.

He wasn't interested in guys. He was just caught up in the moment. He would regret this later and then things would be awkward between us and I didn't want that. We had finally made some real progress with not hating each other, I didn't want there to be this huge awkwardness between us.

Especially because he kissed a boy for the first time.

Why couldn't I bring myself to pull away?

What the hell was it about Knox that had me turning into an idiot?

He started to close the gap between our mouths and I couldn't help but hold my breath. My heart pounded in my chest. I wanted to feel his lips against mine. The need for it was almost unbearable and when his lips were just about to touch mine, the sound of our phones ringing broke the moment and we both snapped back. He was across the room and going over to the coffee table faster than I could even blink.

And just like that, the warmth I felt was gone.

I was back to feeling cold, but unlike before when it didn't bother me, I hated it. I wanted the warmth back. I couldn't even remember the last time I had felt anything other than cold and empty. Knox didn't make me feel that way and I wanted that warmth back, damn it.

"It was Mason. There's another dead body. He wants us to meet him at the crime scene."

"It's only been two days. You said this UnSub has a cooling off period of a week, though."

It had only been two days since the last victim. It didn't even fit with our UnSub's MO of torturing his victim for seventy-two hours. We shouldn't have another body, yet.

"The press conference must have forced him to move up his timeline. He now has to only grab whatever kids are available to him within his victimology. He's like a heroin addict, remember? We essentially just snatched up every drug dealer in town and now, he's craving a fix. He has to get it somewhere."

"And if he can't get the heroin, he'll get whatever he can," I said with complete understanding.

"Exactly. We gotta go, now. We have no idea how many bodies he'll drop before we stop him."

Fuck.

There was no telling what this UnSub would do now. Or who he would go after next. We needed to stop him and I just hoped that in his haste to kill again, he made a fatal mistake that we could use to stop him once and for all.

CHAPTER TWELVE

Knox

WHAT WAS GOING on with me?

I'd almost kissed Ry.

I'd almost kissed a man.

I'd *wanted* to kiss him.

I had never felt like this before. I knew, psychologically, it would make sense that I would want to kiss him. He had been through something horrible and I felt for him. As a human being, I saw Ry in a new light and my mind was processing that. A comfort kiss when he was feeling upset and having to relive horrible moments from his childhood would be perfectly understandable.

So why did I still want to kiss him?

And why did it make me excited to feel his body against mine?

I knew it was a natural reaction to get an erection when being touched on your dick. I knew that. But I also knew that *I* had never been hard before when another guy had just casually touched me or brushed up against me. Growing up as a teenager, I'd had sleepovers and we would sleep in the same bed. I never got hard. I'd never looked at another man and thought he was beautiful or attractive. I'd never looked at a man and thought I wanted to have sex with him.

So why did I want to kiss Ry?

Why did I want to touch him and feel his skin against my own?

I was thirty-five years old. I knew I was straight. I was too old to be questioning my sexuality now, and yet, here I was, doing exactly that. I should be blowing it off as a one-time lapse in judgment. Convince myself that I had gotten caught up in the moment and leave it at that. I shook off the thoughts, pushing the issue to the back of my mind.

I didn't have time to think about it right now, anyway. Not when there was a serial killer on the loose who was not only targeting children, but had made threats against my own life. I had to take those threats seriously, even if I didn't quite believe he would do anything.

Serial killers who went after children never went after an adult. If they were strong enough to take down an adult, they wouldn't be targeting children. Children were easier targets in the sense that they didn't fight back. They could overpower them and that was worth the higher risk of being caught.

We pulled up to the crime scene and climbed from the car. Yellow crime scene tape surrounded another dumpster that sat between two closed buildings, one was a bakery and the other was a pizza shop. Typically, an UnSub picked a location where they figured no one would find the victim until sometime in the morning when the businesses opened. And even then, depending on how full the dumpster was, they still might not have been noticed.

That was one thing that this UnSub hadn't done. He'd wanted the bodies to be found because he made sure that the dumpster had already been picked up and taken to the dump. If the UnSub wanted to keep the bodies hidden forever, they would have timed it right so the dumpster would be taken to the dump and the body would most likely be buried for the rest of time. Our UnSub wanted recognition. He wanted to be known for his kills. And now, he was getting that recognition from the press conference. Every journalist in the city and soon, the State, would be reporting on him and it wouldn't take long before someone came up with a name to call him.

"No Koda?" I asked Mason as we joined him and Jarod. I had never seen Mason without Koda. They were always together.

"He is staying with Lilly for the night to see how she does with having a dog with her," Mason answered.

"What do we have?" Ry asked, looking to get started.

"We've got two victims in the dumpster this time. A homeless man who was looking for some food found them. A patrol officer is with him down at the diner getting him some food and his statement," Jarod started as we headed into the alley.

"Two bodies? Are you sure this is our guy?" I asked.

He had never taken two victims before and it would be unusual for him to escalate like that. Before, he had no real confidence in his craft. You could tell by him changing up the torturing methods. He was still learning. Taking two victims at the same time and having to dump them, it would be a lot. He would have to control both victims and be confident enough that they couldn't escape and find help. It was twice the work and a huge risk to him.

"Both are males, between twelve and fourteen. Both are naked and tortured. Now, here's the weird part. They were tortured in the exact same way, and I mean, *exactly*," Mason stated.

I looked into the dumpster and saw what he meant. They hadn't just been tortured the same way all over their body, but rather the exact same spots. If one had a cut on his fifth rib, the other did as well. He'd made them symmetrical. This wasn't erratic, this was planned and he took his time. He was meticulous this time around.

He'd gained confidence.

"Shit, he's getting confident. He's being recognized for his work, now. He's an artist and now, he is getting attention. He wants to showcase his work more. That's why he grabbed a second victim. The fucker's showing off. *Look what I can do.* He's taunting us at the same time by grabbing a second victim and grabbing two so close to dumping the last one. He's essentially saying, *you can't stop me,*" I explained.

This was going to be bad. With that newfound confidence, his kills were going to be closer together. Chances were, he already had his next victim in his sights and he would grab him before the day was over.

"We need to know who they are. Someone must be missing them," Rafe piped up.

"The M.E. can run their prints and DNA. We might get a quicker match with a photo of them through the missing person's database. They don't appear to be homeless. They are clean and not starved. Someone loved them enough to take proper care of them. They would have been reported missing by now," I said.

"I'll take their photo and run it through the database," Hollingsworth said as he pulled out his phone.

"When's the M.E getting here?" Jarod asked.

"Thirty minutes, roughly. Coop is already going through any camera footage in the area. Both businesses have cameras on their front door, so hopefully, they caught something," Mason answered.

"What are you doing?" I asked Ryzen. He was looking all around the dumpster and on the ground, as if he'd lost something.

"Do you hear that?" he asked.

We all got quiet to try and hear what he was referring to, but I didn't pick anything up.

"No," I said, and I could tell the others were in agreement to me.

"There's a hum. I can't tell where it's coming from."

"Oh yeah, there is a soft hum. Like from a computer running or something," Jarod said as he started to look around him.

I could just faintly hear it. It was most likely nothing, but I had to agree, it was odd that something was humming. We were in the middle of an alley. There was nothing electrical around us. There weren't any machines like generators or air conditioning units that would account for the noise. They were located on the roof of the buildings and even though it was two in the morning and quiet, we still wouldn't be able to hear them. Not to mention, the machines should all be off with the businesses closed for the night. I was thinking it might be a camera. Maybe the UnSub wanted to watch our investigation and see what we knew. It wouldn't be the first time I had come across a hidden camera at a crime scene. Sometimes a reporter will leave it if they stumble onto the crime scene first. The sudden beeping sound snapped all of our heads up. Before any of us could even say anything, Ryzen had beaten us to it.

"Bomb, get down."

I saw the others running out of the alley, but Ryzen and I were on the other side of the dumpster and further away from the opening of the alley. Before I could run, Ryzen's arms were around me and he put himself in front of me just as the bomb went off. The blast was so strong we flew in the air. I could feel Ryzen's arms still around me, but I felt weird as I flew in the air back further into the alley. It was a surreal moment that felt like it was happening in slow motion. When we hit the ground, we rolled and Ryzen ended up half on top of me. Dust and debris filtered down all around us and it was hard to see anything through the smokey air.

I knew I should be sore, but I couldn't really feel much. My ears were ringing and it felt like I was having an out of body experience. Like I couldn't connect mentally to my body. I was in shock, I knew that, but I also knew I couldn't afford to be in shock. We had just been blown up, for fuck's sake. I had to make sure we were okay.

"Jarod! Baby?" I heard Mason yell.

"Get the med bag!" Rafe yelled.

Someone was hurt.

We had to move.

I forced my mind to focus and I looked down to make sure I had both of my legs. Thank fuck, they were still there. I checked the rest of me that I could see and I was happy to report I had all of my parts. I didn't see any blood on me. It didn't hurt to breathe. I was good. Ryzen had protected me from the blast.

Ry…

Shit.

I turned to look at Ryzen, who was lying partly on me. His eyes were closed and with a shaky hand I reached over to see if he had a pulse. I almost cried when I felt it thrumming underneath my fingers. I wanted to move him off of me, but I wasn't sure what his injuries were. I didn't want to risk it.

"Paramedics are three minutes out," Hollingsworth yelled.

"Ry, Knox?" Rafe called out.

"Here! I need help with Ry."

It was only a moment later when Hollingsworth's face appeared above me. He had dirt on his face, but he wasn't bleeding. He quickly began to look Ryzen over.

"The others?" I asked.

"Mason and Rafe are good. Jarod has a piece of metal in his lower left side. AS long as we leave it in, her should be fine until he gets to surgery. Are you all right?"

"Yeah, I'm good. Ry protected me from it."

He finished looking over Ry. "There's no shrapnel in his back. I'm going to secure his neck and then I need you to gently roll him off of you."

"Got it."

Hollingsworth went over to Ry's head and secured his neck with his hands and together, we slowly rolled him over so he was on his back. I was relieved when I didn't see too much blood on him. Nothing to indicate that shrapnel had hit him. He had some blood on him from various cuts that would need to be cleaned and most likely stitched up, but that was about all I could see at that point. I was worried that he hadn't woken up yet. He could have a brain injury.

"Ry, can you hear me? I need you to wake up for me."

I made a fist and rubbed it against his chest plate to try and garner any sort of a response from him. I was very pleased when he groaned and slowly started to regain consciousness.

"That's it, let me see those eyes of yours," I encouraged.

Ry slowly blinked open and I could tell his head was hurting him. He was squinting and trying to keep them open. I could also tell his mind was trying to catch up on what was going on.

"There was a bomb. You protected me from the blast. I need you to stay still until the paramedics come. We don't know if you injured your neck or spine," I explained calmly.

"The others?" Ry asked, and he had to cough around the heavy air that was settling around us.

"Everyone is okay, but Jarod has a piece of metal to his lower left side. He'll have to go to the hospital as well. Just relax, the ambulance is almost here," I said. I could hear the sirens getting closer.

"He set the bomb. He knew we would come. He knew *you* would come. He wants you dead. It's not just a bluff," he said with a rough voice.

"I know."

My hope that this UnSub was just bluffing when it came to me literally went up in smoke. He wanted me dead, which meant I had no idea who this guy was. He was crossing profiles all over the place. He was contradicting himself. He went after children, but he had no problem building a bomb and trying to kill not only me, but the others on the team. He had gained so much confidence in such a short amount of time. It was throwing me through a loop and I had no idea what profile to give this UnSub, now. I was going to need to figure it out, because without a proper profile, we were never going to find him.

The paramedics came running over to us and Jarod. I stayed where I was, but Hollingsworth moved back a bit to give them some room to work. I watched as they put a c-collar around Ry's neck to secure it until he could be cleared at the hospital. They checked his vitals and they were stable and nothing indicated that something was wrong. When they lifted his shirt up, I could already see the bruising all over his ribs. If they weren't broken, they were badly bruised and he was going to be very sore for the next few weeks.

The paramedics loaded him up into the ambulance closest to us and I saw Jarod being loaded into the other. Mason was instantly climbing in behind him. I climbed into the back of the rig with Ry and sat down next to him while the paramedics got ready to transport him. I took his hand in mine as he spoke.

"You need to stay."

"I'm going with you." I was not about to leave him alone and injured in a hospital.

"You have to work the scene. I'm gonna be okay, but those kids are now blown up, too. You have to be there and gather the evidence. You need to see the scene, Knox. You need to feel it. Get into his mind."

"I don't know this time around. I don't know who he is. He's jumping all over the place," I said, sounding completely lost.

"Stop trying to think of him as a box. He's not going to check one. Think chaos. Let the scene talk to you and not the textbooks. You can do this."

"Sir, are you coming with us? We need to get moving," the paramedic said.

I looked down at Ry and I saw him give me a wink. He was right and I knew it. I had to work the scene. I had to see it from the UnSub's point of view. The place was now going to be crawling with cops, he wouldn't be able to get me here.

"I'll come see you soon," I promised.

I climbed out of the ambulance and watched as they closed the doors and drove away. I hated not being there with him. I wanted to be there to make sure he was all right. But Ry was right, I had to catch this son of a bitch. He had just injured two law enforcement officers and there was no telling what else he would do.

I looked behind me and saw Rafe and Hollingsworth. They were both covered in dirt, but they were both determined. Their eyes were hard and I could see they wanted this guy's blood. They wanted to make sure he paid for hurting two of their brothers.

And he would.

He was going to pay for every life he had taken. He was going to pay for every mark on Ry's and Jarod's body. We were going to catch him and then, he was going to wish he never stepped foot in our city.

CHAPTER THIRTEEN

Ryzen

HEADING TO A crime scene for a child victim, the last thing I expected was to deal with a bomb going off. I knew serial killers could attack if they felt backed into a corner, but that wasn't what this felt like.

It felt personal, and personal toward Knox.

He had been a Profiler for close to fifteen years now, so he was bound to have enemies even without going into the field. I knew he'd had to testify against major felony criminals, all part of the job. Any one of them could be this killer.

Maybe the killings didn't fit into a set box because they were designed to grab someone's attention.

Maybe all our UnSub wanted was attention and what better way than to brutally kill a young teenager?

We all had more questions than answers at this point and we were getting nowhere.

I hated this feeling. I hated not being able to know who the target was so I could go after them. I wanted this to end. We *needed* it to end.

I knew the guys could handle hard

cases. We had dealt with our fair share before this new Agency and since being a part of it. However, I wasn't certain that Knox would be able to handle the weight of this case. It was already bad enough that this UnSub had been killing and torturing children. But now, he was targeting Knox, and he was also trying to kill anyone who was around him in the process.

If I hadn't grabbed Knox when that bomb went off, the shrapnel could have killed him. I didn't even think, I just reacted. All I knew was that I had to protect Knox from the hit. It didn't even matter if it killed me, as long as it didn't kill him.

How the hell had we gotten here?

How did I go from hating his guts and waiting for the day he finally got what he deserved, to this?

To me risking my own life just to protect him. To not caring if I died in the process. It was like he was some kind of Jedi and he'd somehow put me in this mind controlled state. I still wasn't over the fact that I wanted him to kiss me.

That I wanted to kiss him.

I was still missing the warmth I'd felt when he was that close to me. I wanted to keep feeling it. All of this was insane and it made no sense. I didn't know what the hell I was supposed to do with all of these uncertain emotions.

How the hell was I supposed to get through this case without constantly worrying about Knox's safety and state of mind?

A sigh escaped my lips before I could tell my brain not to do it. My head hurt and the bright lights in the room were not helping. I had gotten so used to having dim lighting and my sunglasses that my eyes weren't used to the brightness anymore.

It was hard to believe that I grew up in a hot and sunny country like Africa for so long. Back then, I was always in pain and just lived with the headaches. It was crazy to think of what I used to live with before I knew better. Looking back, I was such a stupid kid for putting up with so much shit. Though, it wasn't really like I had much of a choice. It wasn't like I was in a position to tell the rebels to leave me alone or to go off and make my own life. Even though it was hard growing up, even though I had been through a lot, things that still haunted me some nights, I wouldn't change any of it.

I knew, logically, I should *want* to change everything. I knew most normal people wouldn't say they would go through hell again if they had a second chance on life. But everything that I experienced led me here and I wouldn't change who I am now and my career for anything. Working for the FPA had given me a second chance at life. A chance to have brothers and a place in this world. I had been looking for a brotherhood like this my whole life and now that I had it, I wasn't going to give it up for anything.

The door to the room opened and I was hoping it was the doctor telling me I could get the hell out of here. I wanted to get changed and showered. I had a crime scene to work and an UnSub to kill, hopefully. At the sight of Knox strolling into the room, that warmth started to build back up inside of me.

What the hell was going on with me?

"Hey, how are you feeling?" Knox asked as he made his way over to where I was sitting on the bed.

"Some stitches and badly bruised ribs, killer headache. I'm good, I've had worse," I said with a small shrug.

He pulled out a pair of sunglasses and handed them over to me as he sat down on the edge of the bed facing me. "Here, I know yours got busted and they aren't as thick as your lenses, but they should help a bit."

"Thanks. Where did you find these?" I asked as I took the sunglasses and put them on. They weren't perfect, but it was better than nothing.

"My car. I wasn't sure if you had an extra pair at your home or not. Are they going to keep you for concussion watch?"

"No, I can leave once the Doc comes back with my discharge papers. They checked, I don't have a concussion and I'm not at risk of developing one. The blast just knocked me out. Jarod?"

"He's still in surgery, but the doctor did say that he was set to make it. The shard hit his liver, but they are confident they can save all of it. If it turns out that the bleeding won't stop, they'll take a piece of his liver and he'll be on desk duty for three months until it grows back to full size. Mason is in the waiting room. He wants everyone working the case who can. We all need to meet back at the Agency in the next two hours to go over everything that we know and have."

"Good. We gotta get him."

I was happy that Jarod was going to be

okay. It would suck if he had to lose a part of his liver but, thankfully, it regenerated so he should be back to normal health in a few months. I knew Mason would take very good care of him. We were going to get this guy and make sure he paid for the pain that he caused both Jarod and Mason with this attack. The door to the room opened once again, but this time my doctor walked in.

"Okay, Agent Ryzen, you are all cleared. You will want to take it easy for a few days with your ribs. You're going to be very sore. I can prescribe you some pain medication, if you'd like."

"I'm good." I hated taking pain medication. Anything that wasn't over the counter always made me feel very weird. They made my mind sluggish and fuzzy and that wasn't something I could afford to have happening, right now.

"Fair enough. Over the counter pain medication will help take the edge off and then use ice packs to help with the swelling and pain. Twenty minutes at a time so you don't hurt your skin. Any questions?"

"No."

"Okay, you are cleared to head out. I wish you a speedy recovery, Agent," the doctor said, turning on his heel and heading out of the room.

I was already in motion and climbing off of the bed. I needed to get home, showered, and changed, before heading back to the Agency. We needed to figure this shit out and, hopefully, this crime scene would give us something new to work with.

"I have the car out front," Knox said as

he started to walk beside me.

He stayed close and I could tell he was worried I was going to collapse. I was sore, but I was good at ignoring pain. I wasn't going to rest until we got this UnSub.

We made our way out of the hospital and I carefully worked my way into his car. I sat back into the seat and closed my eyes as he headed off for my place. Usually, I preferred to drive, but with my ribs, that wasn't happening so I'd deal. Thankfully, Knox wasn't in a chatting mood and he stayed quiet on the drive back to my place.

We got there a lot faster than I expected and I couldn't help but wonder if maybe I fell asleep for a moment. If I was honest with myself, I was tired. I hadn't slept in close to four days now, and sleep sounded really good right about then. I knew it wasn't going to happen, though. We had to meet the others back at the Agency in two hours, which gave me just enough time to shower to get the blood and dirt off of me.

Once we arrived at my place, we climbed out of the car and I went through the process of getting the door unlocked and the security system disarmed. Once inside, I spoke.

"I gotta shower."

"Are you hungry?"

"Fuck no."

The thought of food had my stomach turning. I needed the pain to calm down a bit before I could eat something. I headed upstairs and grabbed a change of clothes before I made my way into my bathroom. I just needed a quick shower, something to, hopefully, wake me up and get the crap off of me. The hot water felt good as it sluiced over my sore muscles, but it made the fresh cuts sting for a moment. I had a total of fifty stitches in various places from the cuts. They had all been cleaned and stitched up, and I knew they would be fine within the next two weeks. Stitches were nothing new to me. I knew they would be a bit sore to the touch for a few days and then, they would start to itch as they healed. Chances were they were only going to make it ten days before I took them out. Hopefully, this UnSub was in jail or in the ground by the time I did remove them.

As badly as I would have liked to stay under the hot water longer, I knew if I did, I was going to have even more trouble keeping my eyes open.

Turning off the water, I got out and quickly dried off. I managed to get my jeans on before I walked out into the bedroom. There, sitting on the end of my bed, was Knox. I wasn't expecting to see him there and I wasn't certain why he was in my room.

"Sorry, I just know how much bruised ribs hurt when trying to get a shirt on. I thought I would see if you needed any help," Knox said as he got up and moved a bit closer to me.

He appeared to be nervous, unsure of himself, and I couldn't help but wonder if maybe there was more to him being there. We both knew I had gotten my shirt off by myself, that I was more than capable of getting dressed.

Would it hurt?

Sure, but I could handle it.

His nervousness could be connected to our almost kiss just this morning, but he should have been over that by now. We had been blown up since then, and that kinda washed the slate clean. Maybe he was feeling awkward about it all still, though. He was straight, so I would assume almost kissing a guy would make any straight man feel weird.

"That's not why you came in here, Knox. You don't have to lie to me. It's okay if you feel weird about this morning."

I didn't want him thinking that there was something wrong with him because we almost kissed. It was the heat of the moment, emotions were running on high. It wasn't either of our fault. We could just forget it and move on.

"I don't feel weird about it," Knox said as he closed the distance between us. He lightly touched the bruising that went across my left side.

The brunt of the impact from the bomb had hit me there. I had some more bruises on my right side from landing on the ground but they didn't really bother me.

"You could have been killed. Why would you do that? Why would you risk your life to protect mine?"

That was the question, but the thing was I didn't really have an answer to it. It was all instinct and typically, my instincts tell me to protect myself. This time around, all they wanted was for Knox to be safe. I couldn't explain it.

"I don't know. I didn't think. I just reacted. In that moment, all that mattered was keeping you safe. You put a spell on me, Knox. I went from wanting you dead to wanting to protect you," I softly admitted.

I wasn't sure how he was going to respond to that. I figured he would throw out some psychological reasoning and we would be able to move on from the whole experience.

What I didn't expect, was to suddenly feel his lips against my own.

The shock of it had me sucking a deep breath in that caused a sharp pain to shoot up my side. I wasn't expecting him to kiss me. I figured he would sweep that moment in my kitchen under the rug and never bring it up again.

And now, his lips were against mine.

They were soft and uncertain. He wanted to kiss me, but he was so new to this whole experience he didn't really know what to do. Before I could even truly kiss him back, he pulled away and the warmth of his lips left mine. I couldn't help but lick my lips slightly to get the taste of him on my tongue.

"Sorry, I shouldn't have done that."

I could tell he was sorry, but it wasn't because he kissed me. It was because he knew I wasn't expecting it. But he had nothing to be sorry for. I was glad that he had kissed me. I didn't want him to stop. There was literally nothing for him to be sorry for. I could have told him that.

I should use my words and tell him it was okay, but I wanted to make sure he understood fully that I was perfectly okay with him kissing me.

I grabbed the front of his shirt and pulled him back down to me. The second our lips touched, I took control of the kiss. I was a bottom, but I did enjoy being in control rather than submitting to someone. It was different, I knew that. I knew most bottoms were submissive in the bedroom, but that was never my personality.

I had been submissive before, with the first guy I had been with, and I hated every second of it. It had made me feel like throwing up and I never wanted to feel that way again. It was just another reason why I didn't tend to have sex. Most guys wanted to be dominant and that wasn't something I enjoyed, that I could handle.

The fact that Knox submitted to me, that he allowed me to have control over the kiss, only fueled me on. I was actually turned on. For the first time in, I don't even know how long, *I was turned on.*

The soft moan that escaped his lips

was the sweetest sound I had ever heard and I wanted to hear more. I moved my hand to the side of his face and flicked my tongue against his lips, seeking permission. When he parted his lips and allowed my tongue to touch his, I moaned as his flavor burst across my tongue.

He tasted so sweet, like honey.

As we kissed, I felt Knox gaining confidence and he placed his hands on my hips, and then he moved them over to my ass. He gave my butt cheeks a small squeeze and that little bit of pressure forced my hips to move closer to his. If we didn't have the slight height difference, our dicks would have rubbed together.

I was shocked by how desperately I wanted to feel him against me. I placed my hand against his chest and started to push him back toward my bed as we continued to kiss. The second the back of his knees hit the bed, he was moving onto it and laying flat.

I straddled his hips and the new position put our cocks right against each other. Knox apparently needed to feel me against him just as badly, because before I could even move my hips, he was grinding his groin against mine.

We both moaned into the kiss as our arousals rubbed against each other. I couldn't even remember the last time I had been hard, but it certainly hadn't been with any of the guys I had been with.

For a straight guy, he definitely wasn't being very shy.

He ground his hips into mine and matched my pace. We were both dry humping and making out like teenagers, but the thought of stopping made my dick hurt.

"Fuck, Ry," Knox moaned as he broke the kiss.

I pressed my lips along his neck and Knox turned his head to grant me better access. He felt so fucking good against me. Knox was a moaning mess underneath me and it was only pushing me closer to the edge. We were both close and I knew soon enough, we were both going to be flying over that edge.

"Oh god," Knox moaned as he arched up slightly and I knew he was going to explode soon.

His cell phone going off in his pocket sounded like a siren echoing through the room.

Damn.

This could not be happening.

We couldn't actually be getting called right now.

"Ignore it. Don't stop, Ry. So close. Don't stop, please," he begged.

Not a chance. I was not stopping.

"You feel so good. Come for me, Baby. I'm right behind you."

I sat up a bit so I could watch him as he came apart. I wanted to remember this forever. I wanted to know what he looked like when he hit the peak of his pleasure.

Knox gave a deep moan just before he bit his bottom lip and I felt his dick pulse out cum into his pants. I watched as he panted as he came and the sight of it, the feel of his dick pulsing against mine, had me falling over the cliff.

I let out a deep groan as I came hard against him. I placed my forehead against his and we both panted as we tried to catch our breath.

Wow.

That really just happened.

CHAPTER FOURTEEN

Knox

HOLY SHIT.

I didn't even know what else to say, what else to think. That was the best orgasm I'd ever had. That was even better than all of the sex I'd had in my life. He didn't even touch me, we dry humped, and it was the best orgasm of my life. It shouldn't have felt that good. It should have felt weird and awkward, but it just felt *earth shattering.*

O.M.G.

When I kissed him, I wasn't sure what would happen. I wasn't sure if I would like it or not. If I would enjoy kissing a man at all. All I knew was that my mind and body kept screaming at me to kiss him. To see what his lips felt like against mine. It was only a quick peck, because that was all the courage I had within me. I had never kissed a guy before. I had never wanted to, never felt the attraction or the urge toward a man, and yet, all I wanted was to kiss Ry and finally, I did.

It felt good.

His lips against mine had felt amazing, if I am being honest. It was different to kiss a guy, but I was surprised at how good it felt. It wasn't weird like I thought it would be. His full lips were smooth and soft and his five o'clock shadow actually felt nice as it brushed against my skin. I never thought I would enjoy kissing another man, but kissing Ry was somehow better than any woman I had ever kissed.

I'd never questioned if I was gay or not. I always knew I was straight. At least, I thought I was. The thing was, though, in the past sex was just sex for me. It wasn't earth shattering, not even the first time. Sex had felt good, being with a woman had felt good, but it was never rock my world good. It never made me all shaky and left me in desperate need for more like other guys claimed it did for them. I hadn't read too much into it, though. I just figured that was how I responded to sex. Not everyone was a sexual person. It was perfectly natural for me to not be hugely into sex.

A very short time with Ry and I was already hungry for more. I should be freaked out, I knew that. But at the same time, it just felt right. It should have felt weird, but it didn't. I could freak out and deny what I was feeling. I could try to deny that it felt good, but I was never the type of person who cared about labels, or lying to myself. I wasn't the type of person to over analyze every single aspect of my life. I was a Profiler and yes, that meant I had to over analyze everything, but that didn't extend to myself. And even if I was talking to a victim right now, I would tell them to do whatever felt good and screw the labels.

Once I got my breath back, I reached into my pocket and pulled out my cell phone. I noted that the missed call was from Roland.

"Roland called."

"We should get cleaned up and start heading in," Ry said, his voice hitching as he sat up and then groaned in pain.

In my pleasure, I had forgotten that his ribs were bruised, and apparently so had he. I placed my hands on his ass and carefully lifted him up as I got up. Preventing him from having to hurt his ribs as he twisted to stand.

"Sorry, I forgot about your ribs. Are you okay?" I inquired once I got him on his feet.

"Yeah, you're not the only one who forgot. You know, for a straight guy that just ground his cock against another man's, you are taking this surprisingly well."

I couldn't help but smirk. I guess Ry really expected me to freak out about all of it. Though, that seemed like a logical thing to do, but when it felt so right what was the point?

"I'm not going to freak out. Whenever I've been with a woman, it's always just felt okay. I've never felt insane pleasure that takes you to new heights. I just assumed I wasn't a sexual person. But it didn't feel that way with you. Maybe I'm gay, maybe I'm bi, I don't care to label it. I like you, it's just that simple to me."

"I like you, too," he whispered, his voice sounding slightly shy and uncertain, which was different for him. Ry was usually extremely confident. He didn't talk much, but when he did, he had no waiver to his voice.

I placed my hand on the side of his

face, cupping his cheek as I spoke. "Come on, let's get to the meeting and then tonight, we can talk some more if you are feeling up to it."

There needed to be a conversation about what was going on between us. Even if we just decided to be friends with benefits, there needed to be a conversation about actual intercourse and expectations. I had no idea if he was a top or a bottom. I had never been with a man before, so I had no idea what to do sexually or if I would be a top or bottom. Before we could take this further, we had to talk about it.

He just gave me a nod and we quickly got cleaned up and headed out. Once again, I drove while Ry leaned back in his seat to try and ease the pressure on his ribs. I felt bad that his ribs were hurting more because of our time together. He really should be back at his home and getting some rest in his bed, but I suspected that wasn't going to be an option for him.

Ry was used to pain, his body was proof of that. He was also a mission man; he didn't stop until the mission was complete. There was nothing I could say to him that would make him stand down. He was going to see this through and the best thing I could do for him would be to accept that and help him.

When we arrived at the Agency, we both climbed out of the car, Ry a little more carefully than me, and made our way inside. As Ry strolled into the conference room, I made my way to the kitchen to grab us both some coffee, him some ice, and something for him to eat.

He hadn't eaten anything since last night's pizza and that was only a couple of slices. If he was going to keep going, he needed food in his system. After making him a sandwich, I grabbed our coffees and the ice and headed into the conference room. I walked in and saw a man that I hadn't seen before looking Ry over.

"Ice, perfect," the guy nodded as he held his hand out for the bag of frozen cubes. I passed it over and he placed it against Ry's ribs as he spoke.

"Okay, leave it on for twenty and then take it off for twenty. The swelling is starting to get bad and it will help reduce it. It should also help control the bruising. You really should be in bed resting, still."

"I'm fine," Ry insisted.

"You're not gonna get him to stand

down," Rafe simply stated. "How do you know so much about medical things, anyway?"

"He was a boy scout," another man that I didn't know piped up.

"All right, Sebastian, he good?" Roland asked, and I could tell he was looking to get started.

"As good as he can be," Sebastian responded as he moved back.

I handed Ry over a coffee and a sandwich as I spoke. "You need to eat something."

"He's right, you're pale. You need food," Sebastian agreed.

"Knox, this is Sebastian, Damien, and Max. They are from Gaithersburg, where we used to be located. Sebastian and Damien have helped us in the past, and Max joined them this time. After the bombing, I called them for some backup," Roland began.

"It's nice to meet you," I said as I sat down.

I was all for having more help with this case. We were at risk of it getting out of hand, and the sooner we could get this sorted, the better.

"First, let me start by saying that Jarod has made it out of surgery. He lost a third of his liver, but the doctor said the bleeding has stopped and he will make a full recovery. He will be in the hospital for a week before he can be released. He'll be on medical leave for six weeks before he can do light desk duty and then he's going to have to work his way back up to active duty after three months," Roland stated.

The guys all clapped and I could feel

the relief in the room. They might not have all worked together for very long, but they all had a bond together. They were all happy to hear that Jarod would be okay. I couldn't blame them, I was happy about it, too. These were all good men and they were all trying to save as many children as they could.

"I have told Mason to stay with Jarod, that we would handle this. Sebastian, Damien, and Max have all been briefed on the case. Now, someone tell us something we don't know," Roland commanded.

"I ran the security feed for that area. No vehicles were caught on camera. The only thing the cameras did pick up was the UnSub dropping the two boys off, one at a time. He wore all black, had no skin showing at all. He had a full face mask, a ball cap, and a hood. There's nothing I can get on facial characteristics. All I can tell you is that he's tall. Based on the height of some of the objects in the area, he's six foot eight inches. And approximately three hundred pounds," Cooper started.

"Like fluffy or muscle?" Hollingsworth asked.

"He's not the Stay Puff Marshmallow Man. He didn't look like the Hulk, either. So, I'd have to say a bit of both."

"Crime scene has run the bodies for any DNA or fingerprints, but they came back clean. Our UnSub didn't leave anything of note behind. However, the M.E said it's possible there may have been something in the dumpsters around the bodies, or even on them, but it would've likely been destroyed in the blast. Both of the bodies were blown up pretty good," Hollingsworth said.

"We did get IDs on the two kids, thanks to crime scene photos taken before the blast. Facial recognition came back as two boys listed in the Missing Person's database. Brady and Jimmy Johnson. They were brothers and both of them were in the same foster home. Isaiah was able to pull their files and they were awarded to the state when they were surrendered at three and five. They were handed over to a Pastor at a local church. The Pastor stated he had never seen the mother before, but she'd apparently said she couldn't handle having two children any longer. According to the Pastor, she seemed high at the time. He suspected she was a drug addict and the boys would be safer in the system. They were always kept together and placed in the same foster home," Damien jumped in.

"They had only been in three foster homes in the past nine years. The first time they were relocated was because their foster parents were getting too old. They were in their seventies and their health was deteriorating. They made the decision to have all five of their foster children relocated so the kids wouldn't have to see them die. The second foster home was a resting stop of sorts. They stayed there for a couple of months until they were placed with their current foster family. They had never been abused, no files or claims of being treated unfairly. Same as the other children in the homes," Sebastian added.

"We've reached out to their current foster parents and the school. Everyone said the same thing. They were good kids.

Brady looked after Jimmy and they both got straight A's. They never came to school with bruises, they always had food, their homework done. They were clean and in proper clothing. Whenever a field trip came up they got to go. Both boys played extracurricular activities. Brady was into basketball and Jimmy, baseball. Their entire foster family went to every game. Both of the foster parents were distraught when they heard the news of the boys' deaths, and they had reported them missing within forty-five minutes of them not showing up at home after school like they always did," Max concluded.

"Basically, if the foster parents are putting on a front, they deserve an Oscar. They had nothing to do with this," Damien stated.

"Were they thinking about adopting

the boys?" I asked.

So far everyone had been adopted. These two boys should have been adopted as well, but it sounded like they were just foster kids. The ages lined up, but that part of our UnSub's victimology didn't.

"We asked, because the kids had their last name. However, both their foster parents explained that, for school, it was easier for the boys to have one last name. They only had two other foster kids in their home and they'd had them since they were toddlers. They thought it would make the boys feel more welcomed if they all shared a last name. When we asked if they were interested in adopting them, they stated that they had already adopted them in the only way that mattered. Those boys were their sons and they didn't need a piece of paper to confirm it,"

Damien answered.

"These kids actually manage to find a foster home with good and loving people in it, and they get killed," Ry declared with a small shake of his head.

"This world sucks a lot of the time," Max commented.

It was possible that our UnSub thought the boys were adopted and that was why he went after them. It looked like they had been and if he had been watching them, he would know how loving and doting the foster parents were. It could easily be a simple mistake. Still, though, to grab two boys and not just any boys, brothers who played sports was odd. They were athletic. Even at a young teenage age, they could run. They probably could have outrun him, so why didn't they?

"Anything on the bomb?" Ry asked.

"Crime lab is trying to piece Humpty Dumpty back together again. Right now, we don't know much about it other than it wasn't designed to kill a lot of people. Just whoever happened to be standing by it when it went off. The Crime lab has to put it back together to see if it was a remote trigger, a timer, or a sensor that triggered the blast. They are also going to look for a signature to see if we can trace it back somewhere," Roland answered.

"The trick is, with the Internet almost anyone can build a bomb," Rafe stated.

"I'm stuck on the two kids. Two athletic brothers. I know they were only twelve and fourteen, but Roland, think back to when you and Mason were that age. I know you are a good number of years apart, but if you were both supposed to be walking home and a stranger came up to you, what would you do?" I started.

"I'd have put myself in front of Mason and kept walking backward to get away."

"Right, and if that didn't work, you would run," I hypothesized.

"As fast as we could. I'm older so, I would make sure Mason was ahead of me. I'd tell him not to stop, no matter what, until he gets home. Or if we're around houses, to run into the first door that opens."

"See that, that right there. Kids are programmed to run when a stranger is chasing them. When a stranger tries to grab them. And our Perp can't use the line of a lost puppy or offer candy to get them into a vehicle. Kids are too smart. They are taught from a very young age not to interact with strangers. But if they are being chased," I started, but Ry cut me off.

"They run and find the first person they can trust for help. A business, a first responder, or a woman."

"Exactly. These kids are being grabbed in populated areas. It's not late at night, so businesses are open. People are in the streets, but no one ever sees anything. So the question is, how is a guy of a very large size getting kids to willingly go with him without making a single sound. Without causing a scene and screaming for help?" I said. It was starting to click for me. Piece by piece, it was all starting to make sense.

Of course we couldn't find the UnSub, because we weren't looking in the right area. We were so focused on finding this criminal. Someone who would have abused animals in his childhood. Someone who was damaged, but trying to blend into society. That wasn't what we were looking for at all.

"Son of a bitch," Ry uttered, and I knew he was on the same wavelength as me.

"Our UnSub is a first responder," Max stated exactly what I was thinking.

"Cop or a paramedic is the most likely. A cop would have access to the database for adoptions through the court. He would also have access to bomb making knowledge if he studied how to dismantle them in the police academy. But a paramedic would also know how to torture someone without killing them," Roland confirmed.

"All they would have had to do was put

on their uniform and approach the kids. Your mom and dad are hurt. I need to bring you to the hospital. Once they are in the car, they can't open the doors. My money is on a cop. Someone who has paid attention to everything. Someone who has extensive first aid training. He would have taken it because it would have interested him in knowing what can cause the most pain. It would have excited him. He probably worked in the bomb squad or he studied it. Again, not because he was concerned with saving lives, but because it would have interested him. All of the pain and death that can come from a bomb. He would have liked it when people were maimed and not killed. To see them live with that pain. That's how he's been able to not kill until three months ago. He had his fix while on the job. It's possible he's no longer working or he's been suspended. It's also possible, that the violence within his job is no longer enough. He needs more," I concluded.

This profile was now starting to come together. We were finally getting somewhere with this case. Our UnSub had taken things too far this time around and he had made a fatal error. He'd showed us a piece of himself and now, I could use that to figure out exactly who he was.

"He could have been there today. He could have detonated the bomb. He could have been at any of the other crime scenes watching it all play out," Rafe said.

"He could have been the one to deliver the news to the parents," Hollingsworth added.

"Coop, run every police officer and

detective who is connected to the crime scenes. If there's a serial killer who is a cop, there's no telling what he's done in his career," Roland stated.

"Run Detective Jonah West first. He was at the crime scene on the Burnsworth victim. He seemed very interested in being kept in the loop. Often a serial killer will reach out to law enforcement to try and get involved in the investigation as a way of keeping tabs on the evidence."

I wasn't certain that something was going on with Detective West, but it was worth a look. He had been the only Detective not willing to hand over the case so quickly. That either meant he was a good detective, or he had something to hide. We needed to know which one it was.

"The rest of us, we got a lot of evidence

we need to start combing through. We got a suspect pool, but it's massive. Let's start cross referencing the lists we have and see who we can eliminate," Roland ordered.

We did have a massive suspect pool now, but we would also go through it quickly. We had a huge starting point and soon enough, we would whittle that down to a small pool and then, we would find our UnSub. I just hoped we could accomplish that before another innocent child was killed.

CHAPTER FIFTEEN

Ryzen

WALKING BACK INTO my place tonight was a relief. I was having a very hard time keeping my eyes open. I was closing in on day five of no sleep and my body and mind were hitting a wall. I needed to get some sleep.

My ribs were sore from sitting hunched over a table all day. We had gone through a crap load of police officers and detectives, but in a city this large, the number was astronomical. It was going to take a bit more time to find someone that we could use officially.

Detective West was looking like a possibility, but I wasn't too sure. He had a twelve year old son, so it seemed odd that he might be killing young teenage boys around the age of his son. It seemed unlikely that he would be killing boys that could very well *be* his son. He had a lot of experience in the police department. He had worked with SWAT, did a six month stint with the Bomb Squad, and he was even trained as an EMT in the department. He checked a lot of boxes, but I wasn't seeing any violence in his file. He didn't get into fights and everyone said he was a great cop. Even the locals in the bad areas of town had put in compliments about him. He genuinely seemed like a solid cop and not our UnSub.

I sat down at the small island in my kitchen as Knox went and slid the bags containing the few things he'd bought down on the counter. We had made a stop at the store on the way home because Knox had wanted to pick up a few things. I'd had no idea what he was looking to get, but I didn't care too much. I'd fallen asleep for a few minutes in the car while he was in the store.

I watched as he started to look through different cupboards for a frying pan. I didn't really have much in the way of cooking gear. I had two pots and one frying pan. All of which I didn't use. I stuck with the MREs because they were easy and what I was used to. I had no idea how to cook. It wasn't like I had anyone growing up to teach me how to cook and then, once I had my own place, I was gone most days out of the year working for the CIA.

"You cook?" I asked as he crumbled the hamburger into the pan.

"I do. I love to cook. I would ask you the same thing, but I already know the answer," he said, flashing me a warm smile.

"Never really had the desire to learn. I only spent twenty days out of the year stateside. Cooking wasn't a big deal." I shrugged.

"I get that, but now that you don't have to travel all the time, it *is* okay for you to eat normal food. You don't have to keep eating MREs. You can build a life for yourself. You can have a coffee maker and food in your cupboards. You don't have to worry about going overseas at a moment's notice."

I knew that, I did, but it wasn't that simple to change my habits after all of these years. I was used to being ready to leave without any notice. I was used to getting phone calls in the middle of the night and being on a plane within thirty minutes. I was always ready to leave, even now. The concept of having a home, or making one, it was still so foreign to me. I didn't really have a desire to try and figure out how to cook, how to turn this place into a real home. I had more on my plate that I needed to work through, but maybe one day I would. Maybe one day, I would want to make dinner with someone and maybe, that someone would be Knox.

As shocking as that was.

"Maybe one day," I simply said.

Knox seemed to accept my answer as he continued to prepare what I discovered to be pasta in silence. I watched as he moved around my kitchen, grabbing whatever utensil that he needed. He seemed to fit so well in my kitchen, as if he hadn't only been in my home for a couple of nights. I couldn't believe it'd only been a couple of days.

Fuck, it really felt like he'd been there for months.

It was weird how I could go from hating the guy to wanting him around me. He wasn't who I thought he was and that was a good thing. I knew we would need to talk about earlier, but I was hoping with how well he seemed to be handling things, he would want to explore more. I had never wanted to explore something with a guy before, to take things further than a one night stand or a quick hookup. I didn't know what it was about Knox, but I wanted to be with him again more than I wanted my next breath. I wanted to take things further with him. I wanted to kiss him, to touch him, to feel him inside of me. I had never felt like that about anyone before and it felt a bit confusing why I wanted him so badly. Thankfully, it wasn't something I needed to figure out right now. I was too tired to even try and process it all. I had to get some sleep tonight and then, hopefully, tomorrow things would be clearer.

Once the food was done, Knox placed the plates down onto the table. It smelled amazing and I knew it was going to taste good as well.

"Thanks," I said.

He gave me a warm smile as we started to eat. It did taste amazing and I knew I would need to start making a true effort to learn how to cook. Something as basic as this, I could make a pot of it and eat it over the course of a few days.

We ate in comfortable semi-silence. Mentioning bits and pieces of the case as they popped into either of our heads. It was mostly things we had already talked about today, but I could tell that Knox needed to get his thoughts in order and he was more of a talking person. He needed to talk things out to help his mind process the information. He talked a lot, but it no longer bothered me. The sound of his voice didn't make me cringe and want to hit him any longer. He actually had a very nice voice; it was warm and soothing.

After we finished eating, we worked together to get everything cleaned up. This was one of the major benefits of me not cooking; I never had to clean anything. I wasn't against doing dishes, but the dishes I had to do in my day were normally just a mug and a spoon. With everything cleaned up, we went and sat down in the living room.

I was exhausted, but I knew that we needed to talk and I needed to give my stomach the chance to digest anyway. I knew we needed to talk about what happened and I was worried that he had changed his mind about wanting to see where this thing between us could go. I would accept it if he wanted whatever was between us to remain platonic. I would miss the warmth that I felt from him, but I wasn't going to put anyone in a position they didn't feel comfortable being in.

"I think it's important to talk about what happened between us. I know you're gay and have obviously been with men before. I, obviously, have not been. I know what we did this morning felt good. I know I like you and I feel an attraction to you. I would like to explore this with you, but I also have no idea what to do."

I didn't expect for him to know what to do sexually with a man. He had never been with a man before, so it would make sense that he didn't know what to do in the bedroom. I had enough experience for the both of us, though probably not as much as he thought. I could still walk him through it. I had never been with someone who hadn't been with a guy yet, though. A virgin of sorts. I liked the thought of teaching him.

"I can show you. I'm not that experienced, either, truth be told. I've had sex, obviously, but it's never been amazing. Foreplay has never even felt anywhere near as good as it did with you, so I can only imagine what it's going to be like if we do more. I've only been with a few guys since I was eighteen. I've never really dated anyone, or at least, not seriously. Sex just isn't all that important to me. It's been a means to scratch an itch on occasion, but usually, I am happy on my own. We can go as slow as you need to."

"I'm glad I could make you feel good. I've never felt that way before, either. Sex for me had never been earth shattering, but maybe that was because I actually might prefer men over women and didn't know that until now. The best I have ever felt was with you today and I would like to explore that. I know I have a lot I need to learn, but maybe you wouldn't mind teaching?" he said, flashing me a grin.

"I don't mind at all. Though, I should warn you, I do like to be in control. I'm a bottom, but I don't like being dominated."

I was hoping he would be okay with that. I didn't want him to feel like I was going to dominate him and make him my bitch or anything. But I didn't want to feel like I had to submit to him, either. I didn't need to be tossed around and owned in a sense.

"I have no problem with that. I'm not a very dominating person. If it feels good, that's all I care about. I have no problem with control or giving it up. And it's good that you are a bottom, because I don't think I am, so that works out nicely," he said, flashing me a warm smile, a hint of pink coloring his cheeks.

I was glad that he was okay with me liking to be in control more in the bedroom. The guys I had been with before usually had an issue with it. Maybe that was why I couldn't get hard. Maybe that was why I didn't enjoy it.

There was never very much foreplay or kissing beforehand. There was definitely no cuddling or post-coital pillow talk. It was always just stick it in, bust a nut, and then they left afterward.

I hadn't been looking for anything serious in the past, I worked too many hours out of the country and it wasn't like I could tell people what I was doing. I always had to lie about my job or where I was. It was why I gave up on dating and had settled for friends with benefits.

Technically, though, they were really just fuck buddies, because with a FWB you'd usually hang out with them afterward. They knew about your life or at the very least, they knew your real name. I no longer had to travel overseas all the time for work. I no longer worked for the CIA so I could, in theory, build something with someone. Maybe if things worked out well between Knox and I, we could work on building a real relationship. For now, we were just going to embrace this new found attraction and see where it took us.

We sat and watched a bit of television before it got too difficult for me to keep my eyes open. I could tell he was just as tired as I was, so I decided it was time to call it a night and let him have the couch to himself. After all, that was where he slept.

"I'm heading up to bed," I said as I

climbed to my feet, yawning.

"Are you going to sleep tonight? You haven't in days."

I wasn't surprised that he had noticed I hadn't been sleeping. He was always observant; it came with his job. I let out a small sigh, because I truly didn't know if I would be able to sleep tonight. I was hoping. I was begging the universe to let me sleep deeply tonight.

"It's not that easy for me to sleep. Normally, I only get a few hours when I can fall asleep," I admitted.

He stood up as he spoke. "It's common for people who are snipers and have been through trauma. The act of falling asleep brings out anxiety because your mind shuts off and you can't control what you dream. I have an idea that might help."

He offered his hand to me and I easily

took it. If he could get me to sleep more than a few hours, I was all for it. He pulled me upstairs and into my bedroom. He started to remove his jeans and that really caught my eye.

"No offense, but I've tried that before and it didn't work," I said with a small smirk.

"It's not sex," he said, flashing me a grin.

I started to remove my own jeans and my shirt before I closed the door and turned off the lights. We climbed into my bed and he pulled the blankets over us. Then, he was pulling me against him. I placed my head on his chest as he wrapped his arms around me.

"Feeling someone with you, hearing their heartbeat, it can be therapeutic and relaxing. It can help you fall asleep, but also put you into a deeper sleep, allowing your mind to not notice the dreams," he explained.

If it helped, I was all for it. I had never been a cuddly person before, but I did enjoy feeling the warmth that being close to Knox brought me. Being able to hear his heartbeat was actually helping me to relax.

Maybe it was a combination of things, his body heat, the hum of his voice as it reverberated through his chest, the steady, repetitive *thump thump thump* of his heartbeat under my ear, or his fingers trailing casually over my skin, but before I could even register what was happening, darkness descended.

CHAPTER SIXTEEN

Knox

WAKING UP WITH Ryzen curled up against my chest felt incredible. It felt positively right. Like he belonged right there, in my arms. We had both slept all night, he hadn't even stirred and I was very pleased about that. Ry had needed some solid sleep and I was happy that I had been able to help him get it.

Ryzen sucked in a deep breath and I knew he was waking up. I ran my hand up and down his arm as he blinked his eyes open. He looked up at me and I couldn't get over how beautiful his eyes were. The grey in them truly was breathtaking.

"Morning," I said, flashing him a warm smile.

"Morning. What time is it?"

"Six. Far too early, in my opinion."

"It's been a long time since I've slept that many hours straight."

"You obviously needed it."

Ryzen turned and started to press his lips sporadically along my neck as he spoke. "Yeah. I did. Is there something *you* need?"

I was already hard and I suspected that he could feel that against his leg. I could certainly feel his hardness pressing against mine. Waking up with his hard, warm body pressed against mine felt amazing.

I ran my hand down his back and rested it on his ass. Ryzen trailed his hand down my chest and over my still-covered dick. The feel of his hand even over my boxers instantly had me moaning and in desperate need for more. I wanted more than just his touch.

I *needed* more.

I knew we were looking to take thing slow, but I wanted to taste him. My desire and craving to taste him overpowered all logic and all thoughts of taking things slow at that moment. It was consuming me.

I had never really cared for giving oral sex to any of the females I had been with.

I wanted to know what Ryzen tasted like, though. What his dick would feel like in my mouth, sliding over my tongue.

"I want to taste you. I want to feel you in my mouth," I admitted, heat building in my groin and my mouth watering as he slipped his hand underneath the elastic of my boxers. The feel of his rough palm against my sensitive skin only fueled my need for him.

"You sure?"

"Completely," I said with complete confidence in my decision. "Show me how?"

"Take your boxers off," he ordered, and I did not need to be told twice.

I tossed the covers off of us and we both slipped out of our boxers, dropping them on the floor on each side of the bed.

I wanted to see him, all of him, and the

sight did not disappoint. He looked glorious naked. His dick was thick, rigid, and already dripping with precum. We were about the same size and I instinctively knew he was going to feel so good in my mouth. The thought should be freaking me out, but it was only turning me on even more. I couldn't believe I had been missing this for so long. That I hadn't realized I was attracted to men. At the same time, I was glad that my first experience with a man would be with Ryzen.

He moved, turning so he was lying on his left side and we were face to face with each other's hardness.

I licked my lips in anticipation. I couldn't help myself as I flicked out my tongue to lick over his tip, getting a taste of his precum. He tasted like a blend of sweet and salty. It wasn't anything like the musky taste of a woman and I liked that it wasn't. He tasted good and I instantly wanted more.

I felt Ry's tongue run along my shaft and I moaned deep in my throat. I followed his lead and mimicked his movements, cupping his balls in my hand and rolling them between my fingers.

At the same time, we took each other into our mouths and I couldn't help letting out a hiss around his cock as Ry took me right down to the base in one fell swoop. His mouth on me felt magnificent. His dick in my mouth felt amazing. The combination of us both sent my mind whirling and I felt my balls tingle and tighten. I sucked in a breath around his dick, trying to press off the impending orgasm a little longer.

I tried to take a bit more of him into my mouth and slowly worked my way further down his shaft bit by bit. His velvet over steel hardness felt amazing along my tongue. His mouth felt glorious wrapped around my dick. It was so warm. It was unlike anything I had experienced before and I never wanted it to stop.

I couldn't stop moaning as he worked my dick faster. I followed his lead and did the same. I could hear him moaning and the vibrations it sent along my shaft only added to my pleasure. I could feel him growing harder, his cockhead swelling even more in my mouth, and I knew he was close. Just knowing that he was close, that I would be getting a true taste of him, brought me closer to the edge.

Ryzen gave a deep groan as he came hard down my throat. I let out a whimper and then an appreciative hum as his sweet taste flooded my mouth. The feel and taste of him alone was enough to push me over the edge and I followed right behind him, erupting down his throat. The feeling of his throat closing around my dick as he swallowed only resulted in me coming more. This was even better than the dry humping.

He felt amazing.

So fucking amazing.

I knew now, just how easily this could become an addiction.

I swallowed every last drop that he had for me, hollowing my cheeks around his dick, before I allowed him to pull out. I felt his hot mouth leave my dick and I was already missing it. He moved back and kissed his way up my chest, stopping to nibble for a moment on my still hard nipple.

"Well, that was the best thing I've ever experienced," I gushed.

"Me too. You feel so good."

I pulled him in and slanted my mouth over his. The second our tongues touched, I could taste the combined flavor of both of us. I loved the mixture that slid over my tongue and danced along my tastebuds. I knew I was never going to get tired of this.

The sound of my alarm trilling out into the room had us pulling back. As much as I would have loved to spend the rest of the day in bed with Ryzen and exploring more, we had a serial killer to catch. Once we did, though, I planned on spending many hours naked in bed with him to celebrate.

CHAPTER SEVENTEEN

Knox

IT WAS A good six hours later when we
had finally narrowed our list of suspects
down to ten. We had all agreed that we
could eliminate Detective West. Even
though he had the skill set for this
UnSub, his connection to the people of
Baton Rouge, and with having a son,
made it very unlikely that, emotionally

and mentally, he would be capable of harming a child. It would also be difficult for him to go unnoticed in the kidnapping and dumping sites. He was currently being brought in so we could narrow the list down further.

With any luck, Detective West would have some insider knowledge that could help with eliminating potential suspects. If we could narrow it down to only a few, then we could bring them in and question them. We would, hopefully, be able to obtain a warrant to search their homes.

I was willing to bet that our UnSub had some type of trophy. Nothing was missing on the bodies, so he most likely took a photo of his victims and had pasted them in a creepy scrapbook or shrine of some sort that he could then look back on and enjoy again later.

RYZEN

There was a knock at the door and I looked up to see Detective West standing there. He didn't look uncertain at all. In fact, he looked like he belonged up here. It was always funny to me how some people were just born for their profession, that no matter where they went, they fit in instantly. Detective West looked like he had been working here for years with the ease that he had walking around and approaching a room full of federal agents and a few detectives. I also had to hand it to him. This wasn't an easy room to approach. For the most part, everyone was very muscular and looked like they could snap a grown man in half over their knee. West had no problem blending in with any of us.

"Detective West, we appreciate you coming down," Roland started.

"I'm happy to help. Though, you weren't real clear on the phone with what exactly I would be helping with."

I hadn't told him why we needed him to come down. I wasn't certain how he would take this conversation. Some cops believed in the Blue Wall and you did not go against the Blue Wall. The Blue Wall was the protection that all cops had for each other. It was ironic, because so often with a case you had to try and convince someone to snitch on another person. Cops would often try and convince a civilian that they need to give their friend up or talk when they had witnessed a crime. And yet, when one of their own was being called dirty and being investigated, they all clammed. No one would dare to speak out about another officer, even if that officer was dirty. There were a few, though, that were willing to go against the Blue Wall if it meant saving lives. I hoped Detective West would be one of those cops who would only care about stopping this UnSub from killing more kids.

"Please, come in and have a seat," I said, flashing him a friendly smile. I wasn't sure how he was going to react to the news and it would be better to get him in a position where he would be willing to listen.

"Do I need a lawyer?" he asked skeptically as he strolled over and sat down in one of the available chairs.

"No, not at all. We just need your help on this case. As you know, we are chasing after a serial killer who is targeting young teenage males. We have a list of ten potential suspects and we were hoping you will be able to help us narrow that down more," I answered.

"You think it's someone from one of the neighborhoods on the Southside?"

Detective West was very well known on the Southside. Everyone seemed to like him and trust him when he told them that he would get whoever hurt one of their own. I respected the work that he had been doing for the Southside and helping them to trust at least one cop within this city.

"We have no solid evidence. What we have is a profile that supports the actions of the victims. None of the victims screamed or ran away from the UnSub. No one saw anyone out of place at the kidnapping or dump sites. The victims were all adopted, with the exception of the last two. However, they did go by their foster parents' last name, so it is possible he was mistaken in his rush to grab another victim," I started.

"The UnSub also tried to kill us with a bomb he planted on the back of the dumpster at the last dump site. There's no evidence on the bomb in terms of DNA or fingerprints. However, the UnSub does have knowledge of bomb making and how to build a bomb that can be used to target a small group of people. He wanted to kill Agent Hunter but not anyone around him," Rafe added.

"I'm still not sure how you think I can help," Detective West said, and I could tell he was getting nervous about why he was truly here.

"We suspect the UnSub is a cop. We have ten potential suspects that fit the UnSub's profile and we're hoping you might have some insider knowledge on them that could help us narrow that list down further," I finally said,

I could see the shock flicker through his eyes for a briefest of moments before he locked his emotions down. He was good. He had a solid poker face and I knew he had developed it with his time on the force. I couldn't tell by his facial expressions or his body language if he believed the profile pointed to a cop or not. I couldn't tell if he was going to help us or not. I was really hoping he would believe us, trust in our investigation and judgment, and help us find the UnSub.

I already knew the UnSub would be out there looking for his next victim and he could grab them at any moment. He was speeding up his timeline because we'd forced him to. He was also now getting the recognition that he had wanted and he was going to seek that attention even more now. It was why he'd grabbed two victims last time, and there was even more of a chance he could do it again the next time.

"Who do you have?" Detective West finally said, and I couldn't help but let out a small breath that I hadn't known I was holding.

"These are the ones we've narrowed down," Roland said as he passed over the files.

Detective West took them and looked at the names real quick. I figured he was seeing if there was anyone he knew and with how quick he was looking over the names, my hopes were fading. There was a chance that Detective West didn't know these guys or hadn't heard of them. Baton Rouge was a good size town and there were plenty of cops in the city. Not every cop knew every cop. He stopped on Marcus Long's file, paused for a brief moment, and then he picked it up and tossed it down onto the table as he spoke.

"That's your guy."

"You sound confident," Ry commented, but I could hear the skepticism in his voice. He was going to need more from Detective West before he felt confident enough that we had our UnSub.

"Detective Long is forty and has been within the police department since he was eighteen. Ever since he graduated the academy, there have been problems that have come up. I've heard a lot of rumors through the grapevine, but I've also worked with him on a good chunk of cases since I've been a detective and he's not right in the head. He comes across as normal, but I've never trusted him and I would never let him around my kid. There's just this vibe from him. You could feel it whenever we went to a crime scene of a brutal murder or a horrible assault or rape. Where most people are disgusted by what they see, Long wasn't. He had no problem finishing his breakfast sandwich at a triple homicide where the walls were covered in blood. He loved watching the autopsies."

That sounded like our guy. He would be able to work in a position where he could see all of the destruction that he needed to satisfy his cravings. Long had also had experience within the Bomb Squad, so he would be able to build a simple bomb. He hadn't been on any of the scenes, though, but that might be due to his lack of control. If he saw his own artwork, he might not have been able to restrain himself from enjoying it.

"Here's what only a handful of people know about Long. I only know this because I overheard Long talking about it with one of his long-time partners at the bar one night. He was placed in foster care and had been adopted when he was eleven. Now according to Long, his adoptive parents were horribly poor and had to give him back up to the foster care system when he was thirteen," Detective West shared.

Jackpot.

He was targeting young males who were adopted right around the age of when he was given back up from his own adoptive parents. I doubted them being poor had anything to do with it. He would have started to show signs of being dangerous. They would have needed to get him help and not knowing what else to do, they put him back into the system. The system *should* have spotted his psychopathic tendencies and put him into treatment. They obviously hadn't if he was working as a police officer. Detective Marcus Long was our guy; there was no doubt about it, now.

"That's our guy," Ry stated.

"We gotta find him. Is he at work today?" I asked Detective West.

"I don't know. I haven't seen him. We're in the same station at the moment, too. He just got transferred three months ago."

"Why?" That caught my attention. Three months ago was when the killing started.

"I don't know. No one will say why. But

he had been working out of the twenty-sixth for close to ten years. He didn't submit a transfer form. Upper Brass made the decision to move him."

"I'll look into it," Cooper said, already knowing we needed that intel.

"That's gotta be the stressor. Something had to happen that initiated the move and that forced him to start killing. If we can get that intel, Coop, we might be able to better understand what happened," I stated.

"We need everything on Long. We need all the addresses that he could have. We gotta find where he is. I'll call the Station and see if he's in today or working any cases," Roland said.

"I'd be happy to help out if you need another hand," Detective West offered.

"I appreciate it, but I need you to go

back to the Station and quietly ask around about him. See what you can find out. We gotta find where he could be keeping the kids. He could also have another victim," Roland said, pressing his lips together.

"I'll call if I get something." Detective West nodded as he stood.

The room was buzzing now. We had a name. We had a face. Now, we just had to find out where he was and then we would have our UnSub. We would, hopefully, be able to arrest him and be able to ask him why. I also wanted to make sure there were no other victims previously that we didn't know about. Every family, every victim deserved to have closure and only Long could give it to them. We were so close now, and hopefully, by the end of the day, we would have Long in our sights and we could finally end this once and for all.

CHAPTER EIGHTEEN

Ryzen

"THIS CASE ISN'T going the way I suspected it would three months ago when it started," Knox piped up as we got into my car.

"I can see that."

It wasn't everyday that you discovered the person killing and torturing young teenage boys was a cop. Someone who is supposed to be there for them and help protect them. Even though we would have the proof that we needed for an arrest once the warrant came in, that didn't mean everyone in the police department would believe it. I couldn't help but wonder if Detective West would receive some blow back due to his involvement in the case. We would make sure to keep his name out of it, but eventually, people would discover that he had been at the Agency right before the warrants were drafted for Long's home.

"Are you sure your guy can get the warrants?"

I hadn't told anyone that my guy was actually Noah, my brother. It wasn't that I was hiding him from the world, I just didn't like people knowing too many personal things about me. If no one knew about Noah, then my enemies couldn't track him down and try to hurt him to get to me. I suppose, though, considering how close Knox and I had started to become, and I hoped that we could continue to explore whatever this was after the case, it would be safe to tell him.

"He's not *my guy*. He's my brother."

"You have a brother?" Knox asked, surprised. I couldn't blame him. It had never come up, not even when he was evaluating me. He had asked about family, but I never spoke.

"An older half-brother. We have the same dad, different moms. His mother, though, unlike mine, left when she was pregnant. She knew our father wasn't going to be a good dad, that he wasn't a good man. It was fine to have sex with a bad boy, but once she got pregnant, she got her life together and had Noah. My mother didn't have the same belief. We met at his funeral when I was nineteen. He didn't know about me, either. We've been talking ever since."

"I'm not going to lie and say I'm sorry your father is dead. Your brother's a lawyer?"

"Federal prosecutor. He's cleared to operate in any courtroom all across the country. He was the one who got us the adoption files."

"Your team doesn't know about him," he easily stated.

"No. It's not about trust, I just prefer for him to be hidden from my enemies. It drives him nuts that I am so protective of him. He always tells me he's the older brother and it's his job to protect me, not the other way around. I don't want anything to happen to him, though. I couldn't live with myself if he was hurt because of someone trying to get to me."

Knox reached over and placed his hand on my thigh as he spoke. "It's natural for you to want to protect him. Younger brother or not, you are the one with the training to fight. It's in your nature to protect people. One day, when you are ready, I know you'll tell your team and they'll get to meet him. And maybe one day, when you are ready, I can meet him." He flashed me a smile.

"I'd like that," I said back with a small smile as I brought my eyes up to meet his gaze.

I had never had anyone meet with Noah. I had kept him a secret, but the thought of him and Knox meeting didn't make me want to scratch my eyes out. I knew they would hit it off. Maybe one day.

Just as I turned my gaze back to the road, there was a loud crunching sound and then the car was flipping. Glass shattered all around us as we rolled not once, but twice, before coming to a stop upside down.

The world around me was swirling in and out. Whatever had hit us, hit on my side directly. I could feel the door crushed against my right side. Blood was dripping off of my face and forming a small puddle right below me.

I looked over and saw that Knox was okay, or as well as could be expected. He was awake and mostly just in shock. The brunt of the force hit my side, protecting him. The airbags had gone off and I could see there was a bit of burn specs on the side of his face from the airbag powder.

Other than that, he appeared to be all right.

"Ry? Ry, are you all right?" he asked as he looked over at me.

"Yeah. Can you get out?"

"You're in pain, I can hear it in your voice. What hurts?"

I wasn't really sure exactly what hurt at that moment. My body was still in shock and running on adrenaline.

"Figure it out after we get out," I said.

Before any more could be said, though, his door was pulled open. My mind instantly went to someone helping us. It wasn't a very busy street, but a car was bound to go by at some point. To my horror, though, when the man bent down it wasn't a good Samaritan. It was Long. Before I could warn Knox, Long had pulled out a stun gun and hit Knox against his neck, effectively knocking him out cold.

"You son of a bitch, Long. I'm going to kill you for this," I growled out as I fought to get the seatbelt off of me.

Long didn't even bother with responding to me. He was fixated on getting to Knox. He had the seatbelt cut and he was pulling him out of the car.

I had to move. I had to get to Knox and end this. Finally, the seat belt buckle released and sent me crumbling onto the roof of the car. I felt the glass from the windows cutting into my arms, but I ignored it as I crawled across to the driver's side door. Just as I stood, I watched as Long drove away, with Knox unconscious inside of the truck. I quickly pulled out my phone, thankful that it was in my left pocket and not my right, and dialed Roland.

"Roland."

"Long kidnapped Knox. He smashed into our car, tased him, and drove off. Get Cooper to run this plate. JRD 382, it's a white pickup truck heading East on Boulder Ave."

"Copy. Stay where you are. We're on our way to you."

I ended the call. I didn't want to stay, I wanted to go after Knox, but I couldn't. I had no car, and no way of knowing where they were heading. The best chance I had was waiting here for the team and letting Cooper track the truck.

One thing was for certain, Long had made a fatal mistake tonight. He should never have grabbed Knox. Now we knew without a doubt that it was him killing those kids. And we were going to stop at nothing to get Knox back. Soon enough, Cooper would have his location and then we were going to storm in there and I would kill him for taking Knox.

CHAPTER NINETEEN

Knox

THE WORLD SLOWLY came back to me. My head was killing me, but I guess that was to be expected given the crash. I did remember what happened and for that, I was thankful.

Most wouldn't be thankful for remembering getting kidnapped, but I was at least aware of the situation and could get my mind to think clearly. I had to be able to think clearly if I was going to stand any chance of surviving this.

Marcus Long was a seasoned detective and a serial killer. He was going to be intelligent and harder to manipulate. I just needed to bide my time until the team found me.

Until Ryzen found me.

I really hoped that he was going to be okay. The truck hit him dead on and I knew that could lead to serious injuries. The only comfort I had of knowing that he was still alive was hearing him call out to me just before everything went black. I distinctly remembered the feeling of the stun gun against my neck and I figured that accounted for the massive headache I had going on.

I forced my mind to feel my

surroundings. I was sitting and not laying down. I had my clothes on, a fact I was eternally grateful for. My wrists were restrained to the arms of the chair, but it didn't feel sharp. It was scratchy so I suspected it was just thick rope.

I had no idea what Long wanted with me, why he was so fascinated with me. I knew serial killers could fixate on a law enforcement official, I had seen it happen before in my career, but I had never been the one fixated on. Yes, I'd had serial killers contact me through the press or their kills because they wanted to play 'catch me if you can' with me. That was normal. This, this didn't feel professional. It felt personal and I had no idea why. I decided that the only way I was going to get any answers was to actually open my eyes.

The room I was in could only be described as a basement. The walls were made from cement blocks and it looked like some had grey-white mould growing on them from the dampness. The place smelled damp and musty and I suspected that there were no windows down there. I didn't see any from where I was positioned, anyway.

I was, in fact, tied to a metal chair with rope. I looked over to my left and just saw a single wooden door. To my right, however, there was a metal table with restraints attached to each leg. And leaning against it with his arms crossed over his chest was Long.

"About time you woke up," Long said in a gruff voice.

"Long, you know this won't end well for you. You need to turn yourself in," I started in a calm voice.

He gave a dark chuckle at that and I knew he wasn't about to walk into a police station and turn himself in. He was a serial killer, but also a detective. He knew what awaited him in prison. Serial killers also didn't stop killing unless something stopped them. Most of them go down fighting and are happy to die before ever stepping foot in a prison cell. That fight was going to be even stronger with Long being a cop.

"I ain't doing that and you know it. The question is, though, did the big, smart Profiler figure out why him?" he said in a teasing, sing-song voice.

We both knew I hadn't figured it out. I had no idea why Long had it out for me. I had never crossed paths with him professionally. I would remember him. I would remember the darkness in his eyes and how he felt like death. I would have investigated him, silently at first, until I was able to uncover his state of mind. I would have made sure his badge was taken and I wouldn't have regretted it for a single moment. This man was what I'd thought Ryzen was and it sickened me that I ever thought they were the same type of person.

Ryzen was nothing like Long. He was a good man losing pieces of his soul to help keep others safe.

Long was a devil in disguise and he deserved to have his badge stripped away from him.

"Why don't you tell me, Long?" I asked, still keeping my voice completely calm.

"You were supposed to be the smart one. Not so smart now, are you Mr. Ivy

League? Mom and Dad picked the wrong one to give away."

"Are you talking about your adoptive parents?" I asked, slightly confused.

The way he worded his sentence, it felt weird, it felt off. As far as we knew, Long was an only child, so who *was* he referring to?

"No, I'm talking about Mom and Dad. Keep up, little brother," he said with a smirk.

I couldn't help the confusion that overtook my face. I had no idea what he was talking about. I didn't have a brother. I was an only child. I would have known if my parents had another child. I grew up with aunts, uncles, grandparents, and cousins. Not one single person had ever let slip that there was another sibling in my household. There were no photos of another child, nothing. He had to be mistaken.

"Long, I don't have a brother. I'm an only child. You're mistaken."

"Figures they never told you about me," Long started as he moved around. I could tell he was getting aggravated. "David and Moriah Hunter, the perfect parents, the perfect couple. Of course they didn't tell you about me. They couldn't risk having their perfect image destroyed by what they had done. You might not remember me, but I remember you. I was five when they left me at that church. They didn't need me anymore, because they had you now. They loved you more, and when I accidentally killed your new kitten they went insane. Started going on and on about how dangerous I was. They never understood me. They never tried to. I was just a little boy, but to them I was disposable," Long declared, getting more aggravated by the moment.

I knew I needed to speak to calm him down, but I couldn't get my mind to process everything he was saying fast enough to form words. He was talking so confidently that his parents were mine, but that couldn't be true.

I would remember having a brother, right?

I knew if I was two I wouldn't have any memories of him, but still, I couldn't imagine my parents would completely erase him from their lives. Not only their lives, but everyone elses. No one in my family had ever mentioned another child. I was finding it hard to believe that they would have been able to keep a secret that massive from me. I didn't have to believe it, though, because Long did. To him, it was real, and I had to play within that reality.

"I'm sorry, Long, I just don't remember. I wasn't old enough to remember having a brother. I don't remember anything from that long ago. They never spoke of you. I had no idea you were out there. If I had, I would have looked for you."

I would have looked for a brother, but he wasn't my brother. We didn't even look alike. There was just no way. He had to be confused. A secret like this wouldn't have been possible for everyone in my family to keep. Something would have slipped. It was simply human nature.

"They didn't want me. Said I was a danger. I heard them whispering to each other, they thought I was too stupid to hear them. They said I was too dangerous to have around, that I could hurt you. All they cared about was making sure their precious baby was safe. And now look at where we are. Both of us are law enforcement. You followed in my footsteps, baby brother."

"Is that why you called the tip line looking for me? You wanted to reach out and let me know you existed?"

"We have the exact same DNA, baby brother. I didn't know you lived here, but then three months ago I saw you and our parents coming out of a restaurant. The way they were smiling and hugging you. They thought they had the perfect son, but I knew I wasn't alone. That you were going to be just like me. So I did my own investigation and discovered you were an FBI Profiler. You loved death and destruction just as much as I do.

Together, we could be unstoppable."

"You want to be partners. But you told the tip line you wanted me dead. You planted a bomb that could have killed me."

If he wanted us to be partners, if he believed that we were cut from the same cloth, then why try and kill me?

Why go out of his way to cause harm to me?

"I wanted you to get taken off the case so you would be free to join me. If you were off the case, it would be handed over to some hack and we would be free to do whatever we wanted. And I wasn't trying to kill you. It was that other guy I wanted dead. I saw the way he looked at you. He's been infected and I wasn't going to let him infect you with his disease," Long snarled.

"Ry. You were trying to kill Ry, because

he's gay?"

I had to try and catch up with him. His thinking was bouncing all over the place. He was more unstable than I expected and that was most likely due to him having to keep it together for so long. It had to be exhausting on his mind to keep up his persona in the police department for so long.

"He's walking around with that disgusting disease. I wasn't going to let him infect you, too. Now, he's dead and we're free to be ourselves. You can finally let it out. You don't have to keep in all of that darkness anymore, baby brother. You can be free like me and together we can make every parent pay."

"You killed the children to make the parents pay?"

"They needed to be taught a lesson.

They needed to know that if they hadn't given their child up, they could still be alive. Parents aren't supposed to give up on their children. They are supposed to support them and love them. Now, those parents have to live with knowing they got their child killed."

"Because our parents gave you up and then your adoptive parents did the same. It's important that they have to pay for their actions and decisions," I said with complete understanding to my voice.

I had no idea how I was going to get out of here. I was doing my best to not think about the possibility that Ryzen was dead from the crash. I had to have faith in him. I had to believe that he would be okay. That he was a warrior and he could live through this.

Before anymore could be said, the door

to the basement was kicked open and there, walking through with a gun up and pointed right at Long, was Ryzen. He was dressed in his tactical gear, and my god, did he ever look good.

"It's over, Long. Get down on the ground," Detective West ordered as he walked in behind Ryzen.

Long wasn't going to get on the ground. He wasn't going to surrender himself. There wasn't anything they could do or say, he was going to fight. I knew that. So when Long went and pulled out a gun from behind his back, I was prepared for the shots to ring out.

Neither Detective West or Ryzen were going to risk him shooting either of them or me, they had to fire. Normally, that would bother me. I would feel like I had failed in getting my UnSub to put his weapon down and turn himself in.

However, in this situation, I knew it was for the best. Long had killed too many children. Too many parents were going to have to bury their child and live the rest of their lives without them. It would be easier on all of the victims' loved ones if this could just be over. If they didn't have to go through the pain of a trial.

"Are you okay?" Ryzen asked as he quickly bent down in front of me.

"*Me*? You got hit by a truck. You should be in the hospital right now."

He looked amazing, but he also looked like crap. He had cuts all along his face, there was bruising coming through, and I knew for a fact that his whole right side had to be killing him. On top of all of that, he still had the injuries from the bomb going off. He should be in the hospital and not here.

"I'll be fine," he ground out as he cut the ropes off of me.

"He actually isn't. He really needs to get looked at, but he's been refusing to this whole time," Roland said as he made his way into the basement.

"I'm fine," Ry insisted, and before I could even say anything to him, his hands were on the sides of my face and he pulled me in for a kiss.

I easily kissed him back, not caring that there were others in the room. The feel of his lips against mine instantly made my headache go away. Every ache in my body disappeared at the feel of his lips against my own.

"Is everyone in your agency gay?" I heard Detective West ask in a teasing tone.

"It's a hiring requirement," Roland quipped back as his voice started to drift away.

"You got an application?" Detective West said as their voices disappeared and I knew Ryzen and I were alone now. Well, aside from the dead body.

I lost myself in the feeling of his lips against mine. Nothing else in the world mattered at that very moment. We were both alive; we were okay, or going to be okay. We had the chance to explore more of the spark between us. For the first time in my life, I had the chance of having something more than just my job and dead end relationships. I had a chance at something real with Ryzen and I couldn't wait to get started.

CHAPTER TWENTY

Ryzen

IT HAD BEEN a couple of months since we had stopped Marcus Long.

For the past couple of months, I had been healing and spending time with Knox. I had a good number of broken ribs between the bombing and the truck slamming into me. For the past eight weeks, Knox and I had been working on getting to know each other better and not just each other's body. We had yet to have sex and I was good with that. I knew we both wanted to, but we also wanted to wait until we knew more about each other. Not to mention, I was still in pain from my ribs and when we did finally have sex, we both wanted to make sure I wasn't in pain during it.

Today, we had taken a trip to New Orleans where Knox had grown up. We had discovered that there might have been some truth to what Long had said. When Knox had informed the team of what Long had said about them being related, we had dug into it a bit. As it turned out, Knox's parents did give birth to another son three years before Knox was born. What happened to that son, we had no idea. There was no death on record. He simply just vanished. That child's name was Tristian Hunter. Knox had said to leave it alone, and we did.

However, now he needed to know what the true story was. He needed to know for his own closure if Marcus Long was actually Tristian Hunter. And I needed to know if I'd killed Knox's older brother.

"Are you ready?" I asked as we stood in front of his parents' front door.

"As I'll ever be for this conversation," he said, clearly slightly nervous.

I couldn't blame him for being nervous. He was about to ask his parents if they had been lying to him for practically his whole life.

He sucked in a deep breath before he used his key and unlocked the door before walking inside. I had to admit, it was a nice house and clearly his parents had put a lot of effort into keeping it well kept and to give Knox a good childhood. I followed Knox as he called out.

"Mom, Dad!"

He took us to the living room just as his mother called out.

"In the kitchen, Sweetie!"

I followed him into the kitchen, noticing the photos that were all over the walls. His parents had photos of him all over the wall from the age of infancy all the way up to his FBI academy graduation. They even had framed newspaper clippings of every arrest that Knox helped to make all over the country. These were very proud parents and it was clear they wanted everyone to know just how impressive their son was. It was very loving and I could tell that the love they had for Knox was sincere. They were good people that I suspected were dealt a hard hand thirty-five years ago.

"Hey, Sweetie, what a lovely surprise," his mom said as she wrapped her arms around Knox.

"Hey, Mom. Sorry for just popping by like this unexpectedly."

"Oh nonsense, this is your home," she said as she pulled back.

His father came over and gave him a quick hug next and it was all very strange to me. I didn't grow up with love and hugs. Parents showing affection to their children was still very odd to me.

"Mom, Dad, this is Ryzen. He's my, um..." He hesitated for a moment and I knew he wasn't sure what word to use for me. We hadn't talked about what we were going to call ourselves. I didn't care for labels, but I knew it was needed when making an introduction to people.

"His boyfriend. It's nice to meet you both," I finished for him.

"It's wonderful to meet you, Ryzen. I'm Moriah, and this is my husband, David," his mom said before she wrapped her arms around me.

I glanced over at Knox and could see him smirk at my obvious discomfort. I didn't even know where to put my hands. People don't hug me. I don't hug people. Outside of Knox, people generally don't touch me. They know better. Apparently, Moriah didn't know better.

"Okay, Mom, let's let Ry go. He was raised by wolves; he's not used to being touched by people," Knox said, taking pity upon me and guiding his mom away from me.

"Nice to meet you," his dad said as he

held his hand out to me. I easily took it as I spoke.

"It's nice to meet you, too."

"Come, let's sit down and we can all talk," his mom prattled on about inconsequential things as she guided us all into the living room.

Ry and I sat down on one of the couches and his parents sat on the other couch across from us. I placed my arm around the back of the couch as Knox sat close to me. I knew he was going to need support to get through this conversation.

"Those are some thick sunglasses, Ryzen," his dad started.

"I have a strong sensitivity to light."

"Ry has grey eyes and that makes them vulnerable to light of any kind. He wears them everywhere that's not his home, or my home, now," Knox added.

"Oh, you live together?" his mom asked, obviously surprised, but also sounding pleased.

"No, no, we don't live together, Mom. I changed my light bulbs to a lower wattage so he doesn't have to wear them at my place. We've only been dating a couple of months."

"And you thought now would be a good time to introduce him to your parents. It must be going well," his dad said, flashing us a smile.

"It is going well, but I actually didn't bring Ry here just to meet you. I have something I have to talk to you about," Knox started and I could tell he was very nervous already.

"Is everything okay? You're not sick are you?" his mom asked and I could hear the fear within her voice that something could seriously be wrong with Knox. Only further confirming that she loved him dearly.

"No, I'm not sick. Ry and I were working a case a couple months back. I was chasing a serial killer in Baton Rouge that was targeting young males between twelve and fourteen. He had been killing for three months and, by the time we stopped him, he'd killed fourteen boys."

"Yes, we heard about that on the news. We saw your press conference. It was terrible, absolutely terrible and it was a cop, no less," his Dad commented.

It wasn't surprising that they had heard about it down here. It was all across the country. It was major news. It was great for the Agency with being able to be connected to a high profile case. With each new case we took, the greater our reputation grew and that allowed us to take on bigger cases and help more children.

"His name was Marcus Long. His biological family had given him up when he was five after he killed a kitten. He then was dropped off at a church and eventually, was adopted by the Long family. They then handed him back over to the system when he was a very young teen. He was killing these children around the same age he was when his adoptive parents gave up on him. He stated that he was killing the kids to make their biological parents pay for giving them up."

"That's absolutely terrible," his mom said and I could tell she was disgusted by it all. I knew it was about to get worse, though.

"I had the chance to speak with Long

before he was killed. He told me that he was my older brother. That when he was five, he killed my kitten that you had gotten me and you left him at a church. I didn't believe it. I figured he had gotten confused about his biological family. After all, there were no mentions by you or anyone in the family about another child. There were no photos of another child in our family. Only during and after an actual investigation, we discovered that you both did have another son. Tristian Hunter."

I could see the understanding in their eyes. They weren't shocked. In fact, they looked almost relieved. As if they had been waiting for this day to come and now they could finally get it off of their chests.

"We didn't know what happened to him. Though, I can't say I am surprised that he grew into being a serial killer. You have to understand, Sweetie, your father and I tried everything we could think of," his mom started.

"Thirty years ago there wasn't much help for kids who were showing violent tendencies, especially at the young age of three. Tristan started to become violent not long after you were born. At first, we thought maybe he was jealous of having a new baby around. There had been a moment when you were in a bassinet and he was sitting next to you. Your mother and I went into the kitchen to get dinner ready and we heard you scream. We ran out and saw that he had covered your face with the blanket and he had been pushing on your mouth."

"We thought maybe it was just a one-time thing. That he didn't know any better. We made sure you weren't alone with him again. As you started to get older, he started to show more disturbing signs. He would draw pictures of all of us dead. Of him with a knife standing over us. He had started a small fire in the basement that we caught early enough that there wasn't really any damage. When you were two, we wanted to get a pet for the house. We thought about a dog, but we figured we would start with a kitten. You loved the little guy; he slept with you all the time. One afternoon, we couldn't find the kitten. You were very upset. We looked for hours, only to eventually find it in the backyard with its belly sliced open. Tristan had said he wanted to see what was inside of it."

"We knew then that he was born broken. We took him to doctors, we tried different programs with him, but nothing worked. We were worried he would hurt you and we couldn't risk it. We didn't know what else to do. No one was taking us seriously. No one was willing to help us. We even asked our family doctor about putting him in a psychiatric facility, but he laughed it off. Said he was young and just being a curious boy. We had no choice but to leave him with the church. The Pastor said he would be able to get him the help that he needed. We trusted that he would."

I had a feeling they had given him up because he was a danger to Knox. It was the only reason a parent, a good and loving parent, would give up their child. They had to protect Knox and, unfortunately, the only way to do that was to have Long elsewhere. It was a horribly hard choice for any parent to make, but they made the right one. There was a good chance that Long would have killed Knox at the rate he was going.

I felt terrible for Knox, though. This was not how anyone wanted to discover they had an older brother. And now that brother was dead and there was nothing he could do to try and help him. It was going to take time for him to heal from the loss and from the shock that this whole situation had brought to him.

"No one said anything growing up," Knox said with a heavy voice.

"We had told the family that it would be better to keep it quiet. It wasn't that we didn't want you to know, it was that we were worried that you would try and find him. That you wouldn't understand at a young age. As you got older, it never felt like the right time to tell you about him. When you told us you wanted to become a Profiler, we suspected you might find him, eventually. And we were ready for when that day would come. I am terribly sorry, Sweetie. I never wanted you to find out the way you did. We loved him, we still do, even after all of these years, but we were just so terrified that he would hurt you," his mom said with a teary smile.

"I know. I wouldn't have been able to understand growing up, but I do now. And there wasn't anything you or anyone could have done to change him. There was no fixing him. Dad is right, he was born broken and, unfortunately, there isn't anything that can cure that. I'm sorry you had to go through that," Knox said.

The fact that he could understand and

wasn't holding it against them only spoke volumes about how good of a man he was. I didn't know if I would have been able to handle it as well as he had been.

He climbed to his feet, then went over and pulled both his parents in for a hug. I knew that moment was when they were finally going to be able to start healing. His parents had been carrying that secret around for close to thirty-five years and I couldn't imagine the toll it had taken on them both. They were good people who didn't allow what happened to their oldest son to shadow how they raised and loved Knox. They'd raised an amazing man and they didn't deserve to blame themselves for how Long had turned out or the choices they'd been forced to make. Maybe they would have an even closer relationship with Knox and each other, now that this secret was finally out in the open.

EPILOGUE

Ryzen

IT WAS JUST after seven that night when we arrived at the hotel. His parents had tried to get us to stay at the house with them, but we both wanted to have our own space with each other.

The sexual tension between us had been growing over the past two months and it was all set to erupt. The second the door was closed, I couldn't hold out any longer. I pushed Knox up against the door and slanted my mouth over his, kissing him deeply, seeking entrance between his lips.

He instantly submitted to me and allowed my tongue into his mouth. Our tongues danced with each other as he trailed his warm hands down my back to my ass, pulling me to him and bringing our hips together. We both moaned as our hard dicks touched the other's body.

I grabbed a handful of his shirt and pulled him back as I walked us backward to the bed. The second the back of my knees hit the edge of the mattress, we ripped the others' clothing off as fast as we could. Fingers fumbled as buttons popped and zippers swished down.

I tossed my sunglasses down, the light

in the room being kept dim for me. I wanted to be able to look him directly in the eyes, for him to see mine. With us both finally naked, Knox moved his hands to cup the bottom of my ass cheeks and easily picked me up. I wrapped my legs around his hips as he laid us on the bed, then he rolled so I was on top of him. He knew how much I liked being in control and I loved him for it.

"I have a surprise for you," I said as I guided his hand over to my hole.

He let out a whimper as his fingers ran over the end of the butt plug I had put in this morning.

"Have you had this in all day?" he asked, heat reflected in his eyes.

"Since I got up this morning. I figured today you were going to need a nice surprise."

I felt him slip the plug out of my ass, and then his fingers were inside me. I moaned at the feel of the new intrusion, the heat of his skin against mine as we pressed our bare dicks together, precum already leaking from us both.

I rocked my hips back and forth, trying to get his fingers in even deeper. We had done this before, but we had never gotten to the main event. Tonight, that was going to change.

"You're all stretched and slicked up for more. But is it my fingers that you are craving inside of you?" he asked, flashing me a playful, knowing smirk.

"No, I want your dick inside of me. And I want to feel you coming deep inside of me."

He removed his fingers from my hole and placed his hands on my hips as he spoke. "Take what you want. Use my body for your pleasure, Baby."

I moaned at his words. He had no problem being a submissive top and I loved that he was completely open to it. It was freeing to be in charge in the bedroom and it meant a great deal to me that he was perfectly happy to allow me to be in charge.

I sat up straight and hovered over his hardness for a brief moment. Fitting his crown against my hole, I kept my eyes on him as I slowly pushed down onto his thickness. The second his tip breached my hole, we were both moaning and I didn't stop until I had taken him inside me all the way down to his base. He was so big, stretching me to my limit, but he felt perfect inside of me. We had been waiting for months to do this and it was definitely worth the wait.

I saw the pleasure flood across his face at the tightness and heat that my ass engulfed him with. This was only just the beginning, though, and I knew the first round was going to be fast. We had too much anticipation built up to last long now that we were finally together. But the rest of the rounds, they were going to be longer. I was going to draw out his pleasure until he was begging me to come many times tonight. I intended to drain him dry and leave him so sated he couldn't move.

I pulled myself up his shaft until his tip was barely left inside of me before I slammed myself down on top of him. I groaned and Knox whimpered as the pleasure within our bodies skyrocketed. I made sure to hit my sweet spot each time as I rocked my hips at a rapid pace on top of him. He kept his hands on my hips as I bounced on his dick, holding me tight in his grip as I took my pleasure. I could tell he wanted to match my movements, but he remained still and allowed me to bring us both the pleasure we sought.

"Fuck, you are so tight. So beautiful," he breathed out between pants, and I could feel his cock swell and harden even more inside of me. I could tell he was getting close to that edge.

When he moved his hand to grip me in his fist and started to jerk me off, I was in blissful heaven. I clamped my walls around him, gripping his dick inside my heat as I shunted my hips faster. It didn't take long before I was coming hard, my seed spouting out of my slit in long, thick ropes, heat and wetness trickling down my cock and all over his hand.

The tightening of my walls pushed him over the edge and we both let out a loud moan as he came. The feeling of his hot cum hitting my inner walls, searing my insides, was glorious and unlike anything I had ever felt before. I knew I was going to become addicted to this and I was never going to get enough of him.

I had thought sex was never something I would be overly interested in, never something that would possibly be able to bring me this much pleasure, but with Knox it was all I wanted to do. I had a gut feeling he felt the same and I couldn't wait to start our future together. Our bodies had woken each other up, ignited our desire for each other, and I had an inkling we weren't going to sleep again. At least, not any time soon.

"I love you," he said with complete love and devotion to his voice as he wrapped me in his arms.

"I love you, too."

I never expected to be in love in my life, but Knox was impossible not to love. He completed me and I knew he felt the same. I didn't believe in soulmates, but if they were real, Knox was mine and I was thrilled that we had been able to find each other. The future was ours to explore together and I knew it was going to be an exciting journey. Starting with a full night of sex, sex, and more sex.

Who would have thought that a serial killer case would bring me the love of my life?

I already couldn't wait to work our next case together. To be able to wake up next to him and show him off to the world as mine. Knox Hunter belonged to me and I belonged to him, and I wouldn't have it any other way.

Thank you for reading.

Turn the page for a preview of Cooper, book 4 in the Federal Protection Agency series.

PREVIEW

Jonah

MY WHOLE BODY was sore. It had been a long night at work. Hell, it had been a long week.

I hated doing shift work, it was always hard getting used to going from days to nights without much notice in between. That was the life of a detective, though. Everyone had to take turns working overnights so we could all get the chance to enjoy sleeping in our own bed at night and being outside during daylight hours. The trick was, though, when I caught a case, it wasn't like I could just go home when my shift was over.

I worked in the homicide division, so when a case came in, we only had forty-eight hours to try and solve it before our chances of finding the killer went down drastically. Which meant it was quite often a lot of long hours, working all day and night just to try to get justice for the victim. Today, I had been going for thirty-six hours straight and I was in desperate need of some sleep.

It was eight in the morning when I pulled into my driveway. It was Wednesday, though, so I couldn't just head up to bed. I had to get my twelve year old son ready for school.

Andrew, or Drew, as he preferred, was the reason I worked so hard. I wanted to make sure these streets were safer for him, because I knew all too soon he would be off on his own and carving out his own path in this world. I wanted to try and make it at least a little bit safer for him to be out on the streets at night. My greatest fear was getting a call to go out to a crime scene only to discover the victim was my son. It was something I knew I would have to face when his mother got pregnant. I wasn't really sure I was ready to be a father at that point in my life, but I knew I couldn't walk away from him.

My whole life, I had tried to fit within the right box. The box that society said I was supposed to fit into. I had always been athletic. I played on the football team, and I was on the basketball team, too. I loved playing sports, I still do. I was a guy's guy. However, I was a guy's guy who liked to look at other guys naked.

I knew I was gay from the age of twelve. I knew it wasn't normal to enjoy watching the other guys change in the locker rooms or see them showering. I was well aware that I enjoyed it too much. However, I was also well aware that the other guys would never be cool with being around a gay man. I couldn't be gay, not back then, so I did what every other guy was doing. I dated girls. I had sex with girls, even though it wasn't really who I wanted to be with, and I told myself that was going to have to be good enough. I suppressed my gay self in favor of fitting in where society expected me to.

I was eighteen when I joined the police

academy and once more, I was faced with an environment that wasn't open minded and welcoming of gay men. I continued to hide and I even got married to Melissa. When I was twenty-three, she gave birth to my son.

I was twenty-nine when I finally decided I couldn't do it anymore. I couldn't keep living the lie. I couldn't keep my desires at bay. I couldn't keep having sex with my wife and wishing it was a man underneath me. I just couldn't do it anymore.

So, one night when my son was six, I told Melissa that I was gay and wanted a divorce. She didn't handle it well. I knew she wouldn't. She tried telling me that I was just going through a phase. That I was confused. That I enjoyed having sex with her. After all, we had a son. She didn't appreciate it when I pointed out that I only got off on the friction of having sex with her and the vivid fantasies I would have while we had sex. Fantasies of a guy underneath me, whimpering and begging for more. She really didn't appreciate that part. Though, in her defense, I shouldn't have said it, but I was so sick of listening to her going on and on about how I was confused. I wasn't confused. I was just sick and tired of living in that small closet. After twenty-nine years, I had every right to live my life for myself. I wanted to explore my own sexuality, for the first time in my life.

I knew we would get divorced. It was going to be a very easy divorce, because there was no fixing us. I was into men and so was she. There was nothing either of us could do or say that would ever change that.

I had truly hoped that we would be able to co-parent and be friends. I knew it wouldn't be right away, but Melissa had always been open minded and okay with different sexual orientations. She had male and female friends who were gay. I figured once the dust settled and the hard feelings had passed, that she would be okay with me, too. I was very wrong. She was okay with other people. She was not okay with me. Not her husband. Nope. She had never been okay with me since the day I told her I was gay.

The divorce was simple. She signed it almost immediately and she wanted to avoid having to go to court. I thought it was great, that we were going to be able to get along and co-parent, that she had been taking this all so well. And then, it was time to work out the custody agreement and she ghosted us.

She had signed over full custody to me for Drew. According to the document she sent me along with the custody paperwork, she couldn't stand to look at either one of us. She felt that Drew would only remind her of the worst years of her life. Of the deception that I had put her through. She felt like I had somehow conned her into loving me and giving me a child. As if I was some sort of con man using her for her money and a kid. She wanted nothing to do with me and, even worse, she wanted nothing to do with Drew.

We hadn't seen or heard from her since that day. Six years, now. Not a single fucking word. Drew never received a phone call, no text message, no birthday card or Christmas card. Nothing. Having to explain to my son at the age of six where his mother was and why she wasn't coming back wasn't something I ever thought I would have to do.

At the age of six, he didn't understand why his own mother wasn't around. It wasn't like she hadn't been around for his whole life. When she was there, she had been a loving and doting mother. She was always helping with his playgroups and then with his school. She was on the PTA and spearheaded every fundraiser and bake sale. She was an active mom and I thought she loved being a mom.

I knew we were still young when we had him. She was twenty-two, but I figured we both had our jobs and we were responsible adults. I never missed going out to bars and clubs and partying all night. I didn't think she missed it, either. She never showed any signs of missing that life.

But at the first chance she had to leave and wipe the slate clean, she did.

For months afterward, Drew would sit in front of the windows in the living room, staring out at the driveway, waiting for her to come home. The first birthday and Christmas were hard. He was so confident that his mother would come by for them and when she didn't, there was no amount of comfort that I could give him that made him feel better.

That first Christmas was heartbreaking for me. He ran down the stairs Christmas morning and completely ignored the presents under the tree. He sat up on his knees on the couch and looked out the window and waited for

Melissa to come over. When I tried to get him to open his presents from Santa, he refused and said he would do it when Mommy got there. All day, he sat there on his knees just watching the driveway, and every time a car drove by, he got his hopes up that it was Melissa. He went to bed that night crying his heart out and with not a single present opened.

I had to call my parents and they drove fourteen hours to come down to spend a few days with us. Only when his grandparents had arrived did he finally feel like opening presents.

My mom was amazing, because she had brought everything to cook for a full Christmas dinner. It had been a hard day, but we all got through it. Drew had gotten through it.

I had to hand it to my parents, they

were older and they generally had traditional beliefs, but they supported me in being gay. It was a bit shaky at first, but when they discovered that Melissa had abandoned Drew, they were outraged. My father called her a closed minded bitch for not being able to accept me as gay and raise our son together. They were old fashioned, but to them abandoning your child was a far worse crime then being gay and raising one.

We didn't talk about my sexual orientation and I hadn't really brought a guy over to their house. We kind of had a bit of a Don't Ask, Don't Tell rule, but that was okay with me. It wasn't like I wanted to talk to them about my boyfriends, anyway.

As I walked inside the house, I was fully prepared to see Drew running around and grabbing the last of his things. I didn't have a babysitter for him when I worked nights. He was twelve and I knew he was responsible enough to handle being on his own. It wasn't like I went into work at five or six o'clock at night. I went to work at ten and he was in bed for ten-thirty. When he was younger, I'd had a babysitter, but now we both felt he was old enough to sleep alone in the house with all of the windows and doors locked.

I also had a security system with an alarm on every door and window so he was perfectly safe once he was in the house. And he wasn't old enough to go sneaking out at night. That would be something I knew I was going to have to deal with when he was around sixteen. Thankfully, I had at least four years before that would happen.

Drew was also very mature and responsible for his age. I never had to worry about him doing something incredibly stupid. He made it easy to trust him alone.

What I didn't expect to see when I walked into my home was the obvious signs of a struggle. The house was a mess and the further I walked in, the more worried I became. There were lamps shattered on the floor, the coffee table was broken, furniture was turned over, the picture frames on the walls were crooked and some were on the floor, the glass broken. What had my heart stopping, though, was seeing the directional blood drops leading from the living room to the front door.

"Drew!" I screamed as I ran from room

to room, trying to find my son.

The detective in me knew I was being an idiot. I was running around an obvious crime scene, potentially destroying evidence, but I had to find my son. He could be hurt somewhere in my own home and I was not about to leave him injured on his own while I waited for the crime scene techs to get there.

I searched every room in the whole house, but Drew wasn't there. My son wasn't there. I could feel panic starting to claw at my throat, but I fought through it. Me panicking was not going to find my son any faster.

I had to focus.

I had to work the scene and follow the steps.

I had to think.

I had to follow proper procedures.

I sucked in a deep breath and let it out slowly. With a shaky hand, I pulled out my cell phone and called the kidnapping in. The fact that I had to actually call my own son's kidnapping in tore at my heart.

With the crime reported, though, I then turned to calling every single one of my son's friends to see if they had heard from him since last night. I needed to know if he had been missing only an hour or two, or if he had been missing all night. Just like with murders, the first forty-eight hours in a kidnapping were the most crucial. If we didn't find him within forty-eight hours of the time of his disappearance, we might never find him. Or worse, I might find him dead.

I had to work this case, but I knew there was no way in hell my boss would let me. It was too personal. I was too close to it. I understood that, I did, but I was not going to sit on my ass and let this son of a bitch have my son.

No one knew these streets better than I did.

I had informants and contacts in the Southside. They wouldn't talk to any cop but me, and if they knew my own son was missing they would help me. But in order to get them to help, I would need access to this case so I could point them in the right direction. And the only way I was going to get access to this case was if I was working it.

The second the patrol cars pulled in, I gave them my statement before I got into my car and headed off for the one place that I knew could help.

The Federal Protection Agency.

I had helped them with one case two

months ago and they all seemed like stand up guys. They were all capable of stopping a serial killer. I knew they were making a rather impressive name for themselves within their area of expertise. They focused on crimes against children and my son's case was exactly within the realm of their specialty. I needed their help and I knew I would have a better chance at convincing them to let me work the case with them then I did with my own boss.

I also knew they didn't have to follow the letter of the law. They had immunity; they could break the law and do whatever they had to do to get their cases closed. To save children. I needed that right now. I needed to know that someone would kick in the door to save my son even without a warrant. I needed to know that we wouldn't have to wait around for evidence or for a judge to issue a warrant if we didn't have anything solid.

The FPA working the case increased the odds of my son being found and that was all that mattered.

The second I pulled up to the building, I ran inside and up to their office floor. I strolled right into their conference room without stopping. I saw some new faces as I walked by, but I ignored them. I needed to speak with Mason. He was the only person who mattered right now. I knocked on his office door before I walked in without waiting to be granted entry.

Mason was in charge of the Agency and his K9 partner, Koda, was never far from his side. I didn't have the pleasure of working with him on the serial killer case. He had been in the hospital with his boyfriend, Jarod. Their serial killer, Marcus Long, who was also a detective at the time, had been killing young teenage boys and torturing them before leaving them in a dumpster.

The Agency had been brought in by a FBI Profiler, Knox Hunter, to help after he'd had nothing on the killer for three months. At the last crime scene, Long had planted a bomb designed to hurt Ryzen, a man who worked for the Agency and was ordered to protect Knox. In that blast, Ryzen had ended up with some bruised ribs, but Jarod had taken a large shard of metal to his stomach. He had to have part of his liver removed and had been placed on medical leave, followed by desk duty for three months.

"Detective West, what brings you by unannounced?" Mason asked.

"My twelve year old son, Drew, has been kidnapped. I need your help."

I was hoping, I was praying, that he would say yes. That he would take this case over and then I could maybe take a breath, finally. I knew the guys in the Baton Rouge Kidnapping Division were good, don't get me wrong. The problem was, they had too many cases and not enough detectives. The Crime Lab was backed up, too, so any evidence that could help you find a missing child was delayed by weeks, sometimes months. They weren't fast at solving cases and that wasn't their fault, but I wasn't going to wait for months to find my son. I was going to find him before he was killed. There was simply no other option.

"Tell me everything," Mason said, and the tightness that had been wrapped around my throat started to loosen up, just a tiny bit.

Snag your copy of <u>Cooper</u> at your favorite online retailer!

OTHER BOOKS BY EVIE

Federal Protection Agency
Mason
Rafe
Ryzen
Cooper
Noah
Damien
Sebastian
Gabe
Logan

Ruthless Empire
Courting Danger
Chasing Danger
Kissing Danger

Smokejumpers
Hawke
Cyrus
Jase
Gage
Jackson
Xavier

Jasper Springs

Cade
Dawson
Drew
Grayson
Riley
Mitch

From The Edge

Shattered
Runaway
Jaded
Rescue
Hidden
Tormented

Gray Vale Pack

His Fated Mate
His Wounded Warrior
His Healing Heart

ABOUT THE AUTHOR

Evie Riley is a prolific, neurodivergent author known for her captivating MM romance novels. She has gained a significant following and topped the LGBT+ action and adventure bestseller charts with her series.

Evie's writing style often explores dark and gritty themes where her men must overcome difficult obstacles in their search for love, but she has also ventured into sweeter small-town romances, incorporating tropes like enemies-to-lovers, friends-to-lovers, age-gap, and forced proximity. She is known for crafting engaging romantic suspense novels and has a knack for creating interconnected series worlds that keep readers invested.

Interestingly, Ms. Riley has hinted at exploring new genres, such as Alien Omegaverse Romance, in the future.

Outside of writing, she enjoys spending time at the beach and has a quirky personality, described by her partner as ranging from cute to deadly, depending on her blood-chocolate levels.

Evie spends her nights writing bad boys in love, and her days wrangling the sweet boys she loves.

~Evie Riley

www.ingramcontent.com/pod-product-compliance
Lightning Source LLC
Chambersburg PA
CBHW061058210726
48294CB00001B/201